SWEET CHRISTMAS BLESSINGS

EMMA CARTWRIGHT

This is a work of fiction. Any names or characters, businesses or places, events or incidents, are fictitious. Any resemblance to actual persons, living or dead, or actual events is purely coincidental.

CHAPTER 1

*G*reg had snuck rum into the eggnog and while Cerise had tasted it early on and set her mug aside, half of her co-workers at Social Services were not bothering with the usual decorum that applied to the workplace.

Today, on the final day before the Christmas break for most of them, the emotions around the cramped offices were jovial, enhanced by the haphazard stringing of garlands and lights that Greg himself had taken to hanging over the past two weeks in preparation for the holiday season.

It was difficult for Cerise not to be infected by the good cheer, despite the fact that her co-worker had spiked the punch. Carols piped from the speakers of someone's computer and the ancient tree that had probably survived the 2008 recession blinked on and off at odd times, flashing lights in blue, red, and green.

We deserve a little good cheer after the year we've had, Cerise thought, reaching for a bottle of water to drown the remnants of the eggnog out of her mouth.

"There's mistletoe, Cerise!" Greg warned, waving his cup tipsily toward the hanging plant between the threshold leading into Muriel's office. Their boss had the door slightly ajar as she spoke on the phone, her back to the festivities, her body language unreadable.

"I'll try not to catch Muriel underneath it," Cerise replied dryly, flopping into her chair. On a whim, she opened the rolling desk drawer to peek inside, a burst of excitement rushing through her as she saw the tickets again.

"Are you trying to make me jealous?" Madison demanded with a sigh, sliding on top of the desk to sit, her flats swinging playfully as she crossed her ankles.

"With what?" Cerise asked, genuinely confused.

"Seriously? Tickets to Aspen over Christmas? What's it like to be you, woman?"

The question affected Cerise harder than she showed, her gray eyes shadowing as she shifted her gaze back toward the drawer again.

Yeah. It's not as great as she makes it out to be.

"You know how much I would kill to be skiing on the mountains rather than listening to my Uncle Joe prattle on about how this country's gone downhill since Nixon held office? No amount of my mother's dried turkey can drown out the sound of a bunch of men arguing over which ball player is the best of all time while they can't even get out of their armchairs because they're so darned fat…"

Madison couldn't take her eyes off the tickets as if she was going to snatch them up and run for the door.

"Maybe next year," Cerise told her, sliding the desk closed and reaching for her bottle of water again. Before Madison could reply, Muriel opened the door to her office and fixed her eyes on Cerise.

"You. Get in here."

Cerise blinked as the party continued around her, pointing a finger at herself. "Me?"

"I'm looking at you, aren't I?"

"I...yes."

"Come in here," her boss grumbled. "Hurry up. And grab your things. We have to go."

"Go where?"

Madison perked up from her spot. "What's going on?"

"No one's talking to you, Maddy. You and the rest of them are half in the bag already. I need Cerise on this one."

Cerise swallowed a groan, realizing that Muriel was about to lead her to a placement.

"Is it going to take long? I have a red-eye flight to catch tonight?"

"Probably." Muriel smirked. "There's three of them and they just lost their parents in that train derailment."

"The one a couple weeks ago?" Madison demanded, sliding off the table covertly as if their superior hadn't already noticed her sitting there.

"That's the one," Muriel agreed. "They've been in the hospital all this time but they're ready to be placed now."

"It's almost Christmas Eve, ...Eve, Muriel," Cerise said, aghast. She didn't need Muriel to spell out what that meant.

"Yep. And there's three of them," she reiterated.

"Oh my God..." Madison and Cerise muttered in unison.

"Indeed. Come on. We're going to the hospital." Muriel didn't wait for Cerise to agree but she hesitated, staring at her co-worker who shrugged.

"Sorry, Cher."

Cerise pursed her lips, realizing that there was no way she was going to make her flight—that night or any other over the next few days. There wouldn't be any homes available to take the siblings, not over Christmas. There was paperwork to be filled out and signed, paperwork that wouldn't be touched until after the holiday.

The children would be Cerise's responsibility. Her Christmas plans were foiled.

"You want to go to Aspen?" she asked Madison. The blue eyes almost popped out of their sockets with excitement.

"What? No...that's your vacation."

"Not anymore it's not...I'll try to get there for New Year's." Cerise didn't have high hopes for that trip either. Knowing the speed at which the Children's Aid Society worked under normal circumstances didn't give her high hopes for the upcoming weeks and with three children...

"Just take the ticket. We'll figure out compensation later."

Unexpectedly, Madison threw her arms around Cerise, but the brunette stepped out of the hug uncomfortably. "It's fine," Cerise muttered, hurrying to catch up with her boss. "Have a good time."

"I'll send you pictures!"

"Please don't," Cerise said with a sigh. The last thing she needed was a reminder of what she was missing.

Unlike the Children's Aid Society, the Children's Hospital of Philadelphia was properly outfitted for Christmas.

Pretty trees extended toward the high ceilings and twinkling lights wrapped around the railings on every floor. Every few feet, Cerise encountered a nurse in an elf's hat but despite their cheery outfits, the medical staff seemed as overworked and tired as she felt.

It was a thankless, endless job working with children, their plight never ending.

The Hertzler children were already lined up to go on the main floor and Cerise paused, startled by the sight of them.

"Is that them?" she asked, stopping Muriel in her tracks.

"Uh, huh."

"They're Mennonites!" she blurted out, a fair distance from the children, ensuring they couldn't hear. Their homespun clothing gave it away, the little girl's braid tucked into itself.

"Amish," Muriel corrected her. "From just outside Brandy Valley."

The location meant nothing to Cerise. She had not spent any time among the Amish, nor did she understand why their agency was there to help the kids. The little that she did know about the community was that they looked out for one another and surely they had family to return to, even if they had lost their parents.

She voiced her concerns aloud.

"They were on the train with their parents," Muriel reminded her. "We had no choice but to get involved. The middle boy, Daniel, needed immediate medical attention so someone had to make a decision. He's only nine. The oldest, Noah, was unconscious. The little one, Sadie, got the least of it but she's only four and couldn't provide us with any information about her family. We only know their last name now."

"They need to go home," Cerise said firmly. "They have a family that misses them."

"I agree but we can't just take them and dump them in the middle of Brandy Valley, can we?"

No, Cerise realized. *Of course not. There had to be a guardian to release them to, someone to sign off and accept responsibility for them all. There is paperwork to be done.... paperwork that won't be done...not today or tomorrow or the day after.*

"I'm leaving you to deal with this. You must know you're not the only one up to your eyeballs in problems tonight."

"Muriel…"

The supervisor barely stopped, but she glanced over her shoulder.

"Do they speak English?"

"Of course," Muriel scoffed. "Go educate yourself."

Shaking her head, Muriel headed out of the hospital, leaving Cerise to unravel the mess of the three orphaned Amish children.

Slowly, she ambled toward where they sat, lined up on a bench near the door, stiff and silent.

"Hi," she offered. "I'm Cerise Armitage. I'm with CAS. I'll be looking after you for a bit."

The tallest one, a boy of about ten or eleven turned to look at her with dull, green eyes.

"Are you taking us home?" he asked flatly. The little girl jerked her head up excitedly, her own verdant stare widening.

"Are *Mamm* and *Daed* there?" she asked, her accent matching her brothers.

The boy in the middle remained silent, his head staring forward as if Cerise wasn't there at all.

"Sadie, *hoch dich anne*," her oldest sibling ordered, but the girl didn't obey whatever instruction he had given.

"Noah, right?" Cerise asked, turning her attention to him. She knew she needed to get him on her side if she wanted to get the other two in order, or else chaos would ensue.

"*Yah*...yes," he muttered, turning his eyes away. "This is Daniel...and Sadie."

"I'm very happy to meet all of you," Cerise told them. "And I want nothing more than to take you home but to do that, I need to get in touch with your family."

Interest colored Noah's eyes for the first time. "Really?" he asked suspiciously. "You're going to take us home?"

"Of course. Is there someone I can call? Grandparents? An aunt or uncle—"

"Our *onkle*—uncle Abram," Noah interjected excitedly, his face pinkening as if he couldn't believe she was entertaining the idea of reuniting him with his family. "He—he will take us. I know he will!"

Cerise offered him a warm smile, which she extended to the other two children. Sadie sidled closer, much to Noah's disapproval, but that didn't stop his little sister from reaching for her hand and Cerise reluctantly gave it to the child.

"What is Abram's last name? Hertzler? Same as yours?"

Noah nodded vigorously and for the first time, Daniel cast her a sidelong look, but it was rife with skepticism.

"Good. This is good, Noah. Thank you. I'll call him—"

"You can't call him!" Daniel spoke for the first time and his voice was like whiplash. "There aren't any phones."

"*Nee*, that's not true," Noah volunteered quickly. "You can call the Byler's store. They have a phone. They can tell him you're looking for him."

Cerise resisted the urge to shake her head in pity.

How do these people live? No phones, no electricity. These poor kids.

"I can do that," she said brightly. "What's the name of this store?"

"Byler's Amish Goods," Noah told her and Cerise reached into her purse to dig out her cell phone to search the web for a phone number.

"What is that?" Sadie asked curiously.

"Don't touch it, Sadie!" Daniel frowned, snatching his sister's other hand, and pulling her away from Cerise, but the young woman didn't take the gesture personally. She had encountered much worse in her career.

Someone answered on the first ring and she identified herself immediately.

"Hello, my name is Cerise Armitage and I'm from the Children's Aid Society of Philadelphia. I have the niece and nephews of Abram Hertzler here. I'm looking to speak with him if I can," she informed the woman who answered.

"Oh goodness," the woman breathed heavily. "Are they all right?"

"Yes, ma'am. They're ready to come home but I need to find their family before that can happen."

"*Yah*—yes, of course. Do you have a phone number where Abram can call you back?"

Cerise gave it to her and got the woman's name—Sarah Byler.

After disconnecting the call, she turned back to the children and explained the situation honestly.

"We'll have to wait to make contact with your uncle," she told them. "In the meantime, why don't we get something to eat?"

"I'm not *hungerich*," Daniel grumbled.

"Can I have an *eepie*?" Sadie asked hopefully. Cerise cocked her head in confusion but Noah shook his head.

"No cookies, Sadie. We're not hungry, Mrs. Cerise."

"Just Cerise." She grimaced. "No, missus."

She studied the trio. "Well, we can't stay here and there's no placement for you tonight. You're in my care until I can figure out what to do with you and I can't do anything with you until I hear from your uncle or someone else willing to take you. We might as well go have something to eat. I'll need to call my supervisors and see about getting the proper signatures…"

She trailed off, realizing that she was losing them in the technicalities and finished with a smile instead.

"There's a good diner around the corner from here. I don't know about cookies, Sadie, but I do happen to know they make the best ice cream sundaes in the whole city."

Sadie's face brightened. "Will *Mamm* and *Daed* be there?"

"Sadie, stop it!" Daniel cried out at his sister. "They're dead, remember! They're not *cooma* back!"

Sadie's chin began to quiver and Noah glowered at him. "Danny—"

"*Nee*! She needs to face the reality," Daniel snapped. "You can't baby her. She needs to know!"

He jumped up from the bench and stormed off toward the door, leaving Cerise to choke back a sigh.

"Come on," she urged the older brother. "Let's go and wait for your uncle's call."

Noah hurried ahead to catch up with Daniel as Sadie sniffled and remained behind with Cerise, her hand firmly clamped in the woman's. Cerise used her free hand to call Muriel who responded almost right away.

"I think I've located an uncle in Brandy Valley. I'm waiting on a call back," Cerise informed her supervisor. "I think I should bring the kids that way."

There was a long silence as Muriel considered it. "How sure are you that you'll get a response?"

"About ninety percent," Cerise said. "The oldest boy, Noah, is convinced, and the woman whom I spoke with is looking for the uncle now. I expect to hear from him tonight."

"Even if you do, there's no way I'll get the paperwork to release them over the next few days, Cher."

Cerise gritted her teeth, her eyes still trained on the boys in front of her, heading out into the afternoon snow.

"What do you want me to do? I can't bring them to my place, Muriel. There's barely enough room for me, let alone four people."

"I think you should head out there," Muriel suggested.

"To Brandy Valley?" Cerise was dubious at the suggestion.

"Get a room and bill it to CAS but that way, the kids will be close to their relatives and you can still keep an eye on them."

Cerise almost groaned aloud.

"Unless you don't think the uncle will take them."

"No, I'm sure he will but…"

"But?"

The idea of spending the next few days in the middle of nowhere with three kids who obviously didn't like or trust outsiders from their community was hardly appealing.

"Cher? Are you there?"

"I'm here." She sighed. "Okay. That's what we'll do. I'll take them for something to eat and head into Brandy Valley."

"Let me know when you arrive and if you hear from the uncle. I'll start getting the paperwork in order as soon as I have the details."

"I'll be holding my breath," Cerise muttered.

"What's that?" Muriel demanded.

"Nothing. Sounds good. I'll be in touch."

She hung up and tucked the cell back in her purse, managing a weak smile for Sadie's inquisitive face.

"Can we go get ice cream now?" she asked.

"Of course, honey."

She moved the girl along but as she rejoined the brothers, she couldn't stop asking herself one question.

Why didn't I just drink the spiked eggnog like everyone else?

CHAPTER 2

*a*bram Hertzler hung up the telephone and stared blankly at Sarah and Matthew Byler who waited expectantly for an update on his conversation.

"How are the *kinner*?" Sarah pressed when her neighbor and long-time friend did not speak. "Has Daniel suffered any kind of damage because of his lungs?"

Abram shook his head, more to shake off the fog that had overtaken him, the conversation with the solemn-sounding woman still ringing in his ears.

"The..." he floundered for the word, his blue eyes darkening as he struggled. "The *frau*...from the government place for *kinner*..."

"Social worker," Matthew volunteered and Abram nodded, his shoulders relaxing.

"*Yah*. Cerise Armitage. She has them and is *cooma* this way *dienacht*."

"That's *gut*, Abram," Sarah told him reassuringly. "You'll have them *deheem* with you for *Chrischdaag*, where they should be."

Abram rubbed his clean-shaven face, running his fingers though his tousled, dark hair. "*Nee...*" he mumbled. "It's not so simple."

"*Wat?* What isn't so simple?" Matthew demanded, rising from behind the counter to amble closer, studying Abram's face in confusion. The couple had closed the store the moment that Abram had entered, eager to give him the privacy he needed to make the call on the only phone in the district, aside from the one Bishop Speicher kept for emergencies.

"Because of the train accident, the *kinner* have become wards of the state," Abram mumbled, still unsure he understood everything that Cerise had explained to him. "They can't just be returned without me giving my consent to take them."

"But you have given your consent," Sarah reminded him. "We just heard you."

"I have to sign papers...but they won't be ready until after *Chrischdaag*."

Appalled, the couple recoiled as if Abram had slapped them.

"You can't see the *kinner* until after *Chrischdaag*?"

"*Nee, nee*," Abram corrected them quickly. "This *frau*, she's bringing them here, to Brandy Valley. Now. I'll see the *kinner* but they can't stay with me until those matters are officially settled."

Sarah and Matthew exchanged a look but Abram exhaled. "It's better than not seeing them at all," he reminded the pair. "It's been terrible since Elijah and Leah passed. They would want me to do everything I could to ensure we are together for *Chrischdaag*."

"It doesn't seem fair," Matthew grumbled but his wife held up a hand.

"You'll need to get your *haus* prepared for them," she informed her friend quickly. "And for *Chrischdaag*. You can't be ready to host them all, can you?"

Embarrassed, Abram realized that she was right, but Sarah had already flittered off into the store to collect items as the men stared at one another.

"What will you do with the *Englischer*?" Matthew asked in a low voice so as to not rouse his wife's attention.

"What do you mean?" Abram asked.

"She'll be there, watching over you like some kind of spy?" Matthew grouched. "An outsider on *Chrischdaag*? That doesn't feel right."

Abram had not given any thought to Cerise's presence. He had been so consumed with the thought of seeing his niece and nephews again, nothing else had mattered.

"I'm sure she'll be eager to return to her own *familye* for *Chrischdaag,* too," he replied slowly.

Matthew made a sound that told Abram he was not convinced but the single farmer pondered Cerise Armitage and what he was going to do with her.

At a quarter to seven in the evening, a dusty gold sedan pulled up in front of Abram's cattle ranch. The car had barely come to a stop when Daniel spilled out, racing toward the house where Abram stood on the property.

"*ONKLE!*" the boy panted. Abram extended his arms and caught the wheezing child worriedly.

"Shh, shh," he urged Daniel. "You can't push yourself like that, Danny."

With his arm still around Daniel's shoulders, he carefully stepped off the veranda to greet the rest of the car, Noah stepping from the passenger side as a beautiful, dark-haired woman emerged from the driver's seat. Abram was taken aback by the sight of Cerise Armitage. He had expected someone far older, although in hindsight, he was unsure why.

"Noah!" he called out, relieved to see that his other nephew was also in good form. Cerise offered him a tense smile but instead of greeting him, she moved to the backseat to let Sadie out of the car.

"I don't like this seat!" the little girl complained. "I don't like the *kaer!*"

"You're *deheem* now," Abram told her, kneeling to accept the youngest Hertzler child into his embrace. Sorrow overwhelmed him as he took in the embraces of his brother's children.

Cerise stood back, unspeaking, with her eyes to the ground.

After a long moment, Abram rose and straightened his shirt, nodding stiffly at the woman.

"*Denki*...thank you for bringing them here. I'm Abram Hertzler."

"Cerise Armitage. Children's Aid Society." She extended a slender hand, and he took it briefly, but Sadie tugged on his shirt.

"She says we have to live with her now, Abba!" the girl moaned. "I don't want to live with her!"

"We want to stay with you!" Daniel agreed, casting Cerise a scathing look.

Noah frowned and folded his arms over his chest as Abram eyed his brother's children, realizing they did not understand what was transpiring.

"That's not true, kids," Cerise said and sighed, sounding tired, and Abram wondered how many times she had already explained this to them on the hour and a half ride from Philadelphia. "What's happening here is temporary."

"*Nee*! That's not true!" Daniel cried. "I know how the *Englischers* are. They take *kinner* and separate them from their *familye*!"

Cerise appeared horrified by the suggestion. "I want nothing more than for you to be with your family," she insisted. "That's why you're here and not in the city."

"Stop," Abram told the children quietly. "Cerise has taken time from her own life to bring you to me. She is not your enemy."

Through his peripheral vision, he saw her face soften. "*Komme* inside. Sarah Byler made us *nachtesse*. It's getting *kald* while we stand out here."

He hesitated and glanced at Cerise. "Can I take them to *esse*— to eat?"

"Yes...of course," Cerise agreed slowly. "But I will have to stay with them."

"Of course. There's a place for you, too," Abram reassured her. "We have a big enough table for everyone here, don't we *kinner*?"

Sadie beamed, but the boys did not respond as they made their way into the house, leaving Cerise to look at Abram nervously.

"I realize this arrangement isn't ideal, Mr. Hertzler —"

"Abram," he interjected quickly. "There's no Mr. or Mrs. titles in our communities. We treat everyone as equals by using their given names."

"Abram," she agreed, her cheeks tinging pink, even in the darkness. Abram swallowed a smile, amused by her discomfort. "I know this isn't the way you'd expected to be reunited with your niece and nephews but if you follow our rules, we'll have you granted custody in no time and I'll be out of your hair."

Abram said nothing but he could not resist casting her another glance as he guided Sadie up the steps carefully in the low light, the moon the only illumination over the farm.

She is much prettier than I would have expected someone with her job to be. Maybe it's because she's so yung.

"Abba, are we going to live with Cerise?" Sadie whispered when she thought Cerise was no longer in earshot, but the social worker did hear the question as she removed her shoes in the front hallway, her expression exhausted.

"You're going to live with me, *liebling*," Abram reassured Sadie, offering Cerise an apologetic look. "But Cerise will be helping to take care of you for a little while."

"Oh...that's *gut*." Surprised, Abram raised an eyebrow at the child.

"Is it?"

Sadie bobbed her blonde head and lowered her voice as if confiding a secret. "She gave us ice cream for *nachtesse*."

Abram scoffed in amusement as Cerise balked. "I really didn't..." she mewled but Abram smiled.

"Did she?"

"But she did have us pray before we ate it, so I think *Gott* forgave us for it," Sadie added, skipping off to join her brothers at the dining room table.

Abram's heart twinged at the revelation and Cerise's cheeks burned crimson now.

"It wasn't dinner..." she protested weakly.

"*Gut*," Abram announced. "Because dinner is on the table now."

CHAPTER 3

*A*lthough Cerise had driven into the community thinking that they wouldn't welcome her with open arms. She had anticipated a reception as frosty as the country roads that lead her off the interstate and toward the Maryland border as the GPS guided her toward the house on the outskirts of Brandy Valley.

For the most part, the children had been quiet since leaving the diner in Philly but as they neared their uncle's property, she caught glimpses of their heads raising, the familiar landscape piquing their interest.

Now, as she sat at the long, busy table, it was as if she was looking at totally different children, their faces almost happy now that they were in the home of their uncle.

And what a home this is.

From the outside at night, it was hard to see what the farm must be, blanketed in coats of snow but Cerise had learned that the area was known for dairy farms. She didn't ask the children about their uncle's business but it wasn't difficult to figure out as she looked about the house, crates of milk bottles stacked against the walls, farming equipment piled randomly in different rooms of the house.

The man clearly lives here alone.

Cerise didn't know why that gave her a shiver of pleasure but she quickly dismissed it as she pecked at the casserole on her plate. Contrary to what she'd told Abram, she had filled up on ice cream, even if the children appeared to still be hungry.

"You don't need to be shy," Abram encouraged her, but before she could respond, there was a knock on the door. Abram rose as Noah glanced up from his plate.

"That will be Joshua," he informed the children.

"Joshua?" Cerise asked before she could stop herself. She felt as though she should be taking notes of all the people coming and going but Abram was already gone, answering the door as she eyed the children curiously. Daniel refused to meet her gaze but Noah offered her a sidelong look.

"He was our closest neighbor…" The boy faltered. "He was an *Englisher* once."

Shocked, Cerise looked up as an older man with silvery-blond hair and a full beard entered the dining room, Abram on his heels. He didn't look like a city person to Cerise and he eyed her with the same skepticism the children had at first glance.

"*Hallo*," the newcomer said. "I'm Joshua."

Cerise started to stand but Joshua held out his hands. "Sit. *Esse*—eat."

She reclaimed her seat and studied the man as Abram took his chair again at the head of the table.

Joshua turned his attention to the children who smiled tentatively at him. "*Hallo, kinner*. Bishop Speicher will *komme* by tomorrow to check on you."

None of the children responded.

"Are you well?" Joshua pressed. "Did they treat you well at the hospital?"

"*Yah*," Noah said quickly.

"We have to stay with her," Daniel spat out. "We can't stay here."

"Stop it, Danny," Noah interjected, surprising the CAS worker. "She doesn't want to be here either."

All eyes were on Cerise now whose own eyes widened in dismay. "Th-that's not true," she sputtered. "I want to make sure you're safe and cared for."

"I just mean that it's *Chrischdaag*," Noah said. "You have your own *familye*. You don't want to spend it with *fremmer*—strangers."

"Oh." Cerise chuckled nervously and stared down at the table, shaking her head. She felt Joshua's hazel gaze boring into her. "That's not true, actually. I-I don't have a family."

"Everyone has a *familye*," Sadie insisted, not believing her. "You're just being nice."

Cerise raise her dark head of hair and met the little girl's indignant stare. "No. I really don't. I...I grew up in foster care..."

She bit on her lower lip, unsure if the girl was too young to understand what she was saying but Noah clucked his tongue.

"You're an orphan?"

Cerise shrugged and nodded. "I was left at a firehall when I was born. I never knew my parents."

"Oh, that's so sad!" Sadie cried but Cerise shook her head vehemently.

"Please don't be sad for me. I made lots of different brothers and sisters over the years," she went on in a rush, trying to sound more cheerful than she felt. "It was a big adventure."

"What were you going to do for the holiday season?" Abram asked.

"Not much," Cerise fibbed, not wanting to make the family feel guilty for altering her plans. "Sometimes I go away somewhere but this year…"

She shrugged indifferently.

Joshua made a commiserating sound but when Cerise glanced back at him, he had turned away.

"Hoch dich anne, Josh. Esse."

"Nee, nee," Joshua waved his hand. "Lydia and I had *nachtesse* already, but Sarah and Matthew told me that the *kinner* were *cooma* home *dienacht.* I wanted to stop by and see them myself. I didn't realize you had company. I'll be going now."

"Maybe we'll see you in the *mariye, yah?"* Abram said, rising to see his friend out. Joshua gave Cerise a look before allowing Abram to lead him back out toward the front door.

"He used to live in the city?" Cerise asked in disbelief as the men wandered out of earshot.

"Yah," Noah replied. "He was a minister there, too…"

"He's a minister here?" Cerise pressed, unsure why she was so fascinated with all this information.

The oldest boy nodded.

That's probably why they accepted him into the community, Cerise thought wistfully. Again, she was surprised by her feelings.

It's been a long day. I need to get some rest.

Abram returned, a small smile toying on his lips.

"Josh thinks you should join us tomorrow for the singings," he informed her. She stared at him blankly and he chuckled. "I forget that you know nothing about our customs. Somehow it feels like you know about our ways already."

Cerise was inexplicably flattered by his words. "I'm sorry to disappoint you but I really don't know anything about your life. But I would love to learn."

"*Gut.* Then I can count you in for tomorrow."

Cerise paled and glanced at the children who had finally stopped eating but their eyes had glazed over, their ears clearly closed to the conversation as sleepiness took hold.

"Are you sure that's a good idea?" she asked slowly. "I mean… am I allowed to just wander around here?"

Abram frowned lightly. "You won't be 'wandering around' but why wouldn't you be?"

Embarrassed, Cerise shrugged slightly. "I don't know. I always thought that your community was very…close knit. That you didn't take well to outsiders."

"Joshua used to be an *Englischer.*"

"Noah just told me that. It's hard to believe."

"Why?" Abram asked curiously. "Does our life seem so different?"

Cerise opened her mouth to say "yes!" but she faltered. Her head raised to peer around the pretty but ill-kept house. The lack of electricity was barely noticeable with the kerosene lamps and fireplace going. It was warm and cozy inside, the place as comfortable as any house she had ever lived in.

Better than some of the foster families I've dealt with.

Her stare moved to the half-slumbering children who were full-bellied and contented. Their fear had appeared to have dissipated the moment they had crossed the threshold.

"No," she murmured, mortified by her generalization of the Amish and how little she had known about them. "It doesn't seem that different."

"Let us show you around over the next few days," Abram pressed. "Since you're here, anyway. You might as well make the most of it."

"I-I'd like that," Cerise agreed but even as she said yes, she wasn't sure if she was looking forward to learning about the Amish or hanging out with the handsome Abram Hertzler.

"I should take the kids back to the motel," she added, standing abruptly as a hot blush hit her cheeks.

"There's plenty of room here if you'd prefer to stay here tonight," Abram offered softly. Cerise cringed, waiting for the children to begin clamoring in agreement but to her surprise, none of them did.

"I really can't, Abram," she mumbled, shamed at how much she wanted to. "I-I have to take them back with me."

"I understand and I respect what you have to do." She met his gaze and saw that he was being sincere. "*Thank* you for keeping my brother's children safe, Cerise."

"I'm just doing my job," she told him, standing and shifting her eyes away.

"Somehow I think you are going above and beyond for your job," he insisted. Clearing his throat, he woke the kids from their semi-trance and informed them that it was time to go.

The complaints began then.

"Can't we stay *dienacht*?"

"It's so late!"

"Why do we have to go, Abba?"

"I want all three of you to be on your best behavior for Cerise," Abram warned them. "You remember that she's a long way from home too, *yah*? Soon, we will all be under the same roof, but for now, we have to do it this way. Don't give her any trouble, *yah*?"

Begrudgingly, they agreed and followed Cerise to the door. It wasn't until she was putting her boots on that she thought of the dishes.

"Oh! I can't leave you with that mess!"

"It's all right. I've been doing this myself for a long while. I can manage," he promised, ushering her onto the porch.

We both know what it's like to be alone. I wonder how he's going to fare with three new bodies running around.

Cerise wondered if she wasn't the slightest bit jealous.

CHAPTER 4

*O*n the day before Christmas Eve, many events had been planned within the tiny district for the upcoming festive season, but there was still work to be done.

Cattle farming was not like crop farming and continued year-round for men like Abram who still woke pre-dawn to tend to his livestock, ensuring they were milked, fed and warm enough for the day ahead.

It had turned warmer overnight, melting some of the hardened snow that had covered the Pennsylvania landscape over the past couple of weeks. Abram could not help but feel as if Cerise had brought along the heat with her sweetness, despite the lateness of December.

Still, he hoped for a white Christmas for the children's sake and hurried along through his chores before they arrived that morning. He did not want to be distracted when his nephews and niece appeared, but it proved to be a futile wish. There was just too much to do.

When Cerise's gold sedan drove back up over the slushy driveway just after nine a.m., the children piled out of the vehicle, sloshing through the sleet to wet their pants and slip over in the icy conditions. Abram rushed over to meet them, still in the midst of his work day.

He had hoped to tidy up his house before they came, but now that was hopeless as well.

"You're here already!" he called out, unable to keep the mild frustration from his voice. Surprised, Cerise stared at him, confused by his tone.

"Didn't you say nine o'clock yesterday?" she asked, glancing at her cell phone. "Did I get the time wrong?"

Sheepishly, Abram shook his head, hanging his chin. "*Nee*—no," he replied apologetically. "There's just so much to do and I'm not prepared."

"Oh," Cerise said slowly, looking around, her lovely eyes widening in appreciation as she took in the land for the first time in the daylight. "Yes, you really do have your hands full out here, don't you?"

He chuckled dryly. "It's a lot of *warrick*—uh, work, without three *kinner*, children," he muttered, forgetting not to mix his Pennsylvania Dutch with English in his flustered state.

She smiled patiently as the children disappeared into the house. "First off, you don't have to translate for me. I speak Spanish already so I have a bit of an aptitude for picking up languages. I can figure out what you're trying to say—even if it takes me a second sometimes. And secondly, I'm here. I can give you a hand if you tell me what you need. I'm not doing much just standing around, am I?"

Abram found himself staring at her in awe. He had not expected any of the words to come out of her mouth that had and yet he was not surprised by them.

She is very special. Gott has brought her here for a reason.

"If you could just mind the *kinner* until I'm finished here. I'll make something to *esse* when I'm done and we'll join the others for the singings."

Cerise's mouth parted as if she were going to say something but changed her mind last minute. "That's fine," she agreed instead. "You do what you have to do. We're fine."

Abram nodded gratefully and turned back to his cattle as she headed to join the children in the house.

He rushed through the rest of his chores as fast as he could, suddenly realizing how long things took. It had never been of much consequence to him before, but now that he had others waiting on him, he recognized just how long his duties took, particularly in the winter months with the cold slowing him down.

An hour later, he trudged through the back door, pounding the snow off his boots, his hands freezing under his gloves in spite of the bright sunshine pouring down overhead.

His nose was immediately overpowered by the scent of bacon.

Blinking, Abram looked around the spotless kitchen. No one was there, but the dishes were washed, and the once untidy area had been put in order, floors washed, and counters scrubbed.

"*Hallo?*" he called out, slipping out of his sopping wet boots and coat.

"We're in the dining room," Cerise called out. "Come and... *esse.*"

The children giggled at her use of their native tongue and Abram cautiously wandered toward the sound of their voices, his eyes growing wider by the second. It was not just the kitchen that Cerise had cleaned but the main floor entirely—after or before preparing breakfast, he couldn't say.

"I hope you don't mind," she said nervously, catching his disbelieving stare as he gawked at the spread on the table. "The kids didn't much care for the cereal at the motel this morning."

"That's not *mariyeesse,*" Noah insisted. "Breakfast is supposed to be hot. *Daed* always said it was the most important meal because it's what gets you through the day."

"Your dad was absolutely right," Cerise agreed, looking down guiltily. "But as you know, there's not much in the way of a kitchen at the motel..."

"This is *wunderbar,*" Abram told her earnestly, taking his place at the head of the table.

"We waited as long as we could for you but the kids were hungry," Cerise went on apologetically.

"We prayed," Noah added quickly, eying his uncle. "Before we ate."

"We did," Cerise confirmed. "We wouldn't eat otherwise."

"You also cleaned the *haus,*" Abram commented, nodding around vaguely. Cerise blushed across the table.

"I tidied up a bit while I was cooking," she admitted. "I wouldn't say I *cleaned...*"

"I helped!" Sadie chimed in.

"She did," Cerise agreed. "And Daniel was kind enough to show me where some of the supplies were."

She smiled at the still sullen middle child but Abram noticed that he looked pleased with her compliment.

"It was definitely a team effort."

"It looks *wunderbar* and smells *wunderbar*," Abram confirmed, his stomach growling at the sight of the eggs and bread in front of him.

"Dig in," Cerise encouraged. "I hope it's not too cold."

Abram ate with gusto, relishing every morsel that Cerise had created and moving in for seconds as the children laughed.

"You were *hungerich*!" Sadie chortled, pointing at him. Abram finally put his fork down and sighed with contentment, offering Cerise a warm smile.

"I didn't realize just how hungry I was," he admitted. "*Denki*, Cerise."

"She's a *gut koch*," Daniel said unexpectedly, and Abram watched as the woman blushed with pleasure.

She stood and began collecting the dishes to wash, Sadie jumping up to help without being asked and the boys remained at the table with their uncle. When she was out of earshot, he turned to them.

"How was the hotel last night?" he asked them honestly.

Noah shrugged as Daniel frowned.

"Uncomfortable," Daniel grumbled. "I missed my bed."

A pang of sympathy touched Abram's heart. He wondered if Daniel understood that he was never returning to his own bed, that the house where he and his siblings had been raised would be sold and that his belongings would be going into storage until Abram could sort though and figure out what would fit in his own modest place.

He said none of this to the boys.

"Cerise is very kind," Noah added, reading his uncle's worried expression. "Sadie likes her a lot."

"She seems like a *gut frau*," Abram agreed. "Despite what she said about not having *familye*, she must have people who miss her in the city. She is still away from her home."

The boys hung their heads in shame and more guilt flooded Abram. He had not meant to make them feel bad. But before he could apologize, Cerise returned and flashed her pretty smile at them.

"What time is Joshua expecting us?"

Abram blinked, temporarily confused by her question until she elaborated. "You said there's an event today?"

"Oh! The singings. I almost forgot!"

He stood and brushed the crumbs from his shirt. "We should get going now. We're already late. Leave the dishes and get your coats. Noah, go get the buggy ready."

The district in Brandy Valley had only thirty families but Bishop Speicher had high hopes for the upcoming years as many from Lancaster County moved south to join.

Abram hoped it would never grow too large, the small population one of the things that he liked so much about the area, along with their more liberal following of the Ordnung.

But with that also came more gossip and bringing Cerise to the community's hymnals almost cut the singing off mid-choir. The whispers erupted through the crowd like a wave.

"I probably shouldn't have come," Cerise mumbled as they dismounted the buggy, her arms wrapping around her body.

"Nonsense. The children want you here, don't you, *kinner*?"

"*Yah!*" Sadie squeaked, grabbing her hand. "*Komme.* The *weiwer* are on this side."

Cerise looked at Abram in confusion and he explained. "Men and women are separate during services but we'll reconvene afterward for food and socializing. You'll be fine."

Aghast, Cerise's eyes popped but she allowed Sadie to pull her toward the women's section, her gaze still trained on him. Abram swallowed a smile, unable to overcome his amusement at the newcomer. He tried to envision himself seeing the Amish community for the first time and how strange it must be for an Englischer. His own Rumspringa had been brief, his interest in the English world nil.

With Noah and Daniel at his side, he found Matthew Byler near the front of the service and the two shared a hymn book.

"Is that the social worker?" Matthew asked in a low whisper, under the chorus of voices. Abram nodded, sneaking another peek at Cerise. Sadie had shown her the book and the women around her gawked at the Englisher, as if she was an alien.

"How is she getting along with you?"

"Wonderfully," Abram blurted out before he could stop himself.

The shopkeeper's eyebrows shot up in shock.

"*Yah?*"

But Abram felt no shame for his admission and nodded again. Keeping his voice low to ensure that the other men did not overhear them, he told his friend the truth.

"She has been nothing but gentle and caring to the *kinner* since her arrival. She has no *familye* of her own and I suspect she gave up her own plans to be here. She's a *gut*, Christian *frau*, selfless…"

He paused and raised his head, eyes falling on Joshua who stood up front with the other ministers and Bishop Speicher.

"I think she would make a fine addition to our community."

"*WAT?!*"

Embarrassed, Matthew lowered his voice and nodded apologetically at the frowning faces around him. Clearing his throat, he turned his attention back toward his friend. "She's an *Englischer!*" he hissed.

"So was Joshua."

"But…he was already a minister."

"And she works with *kinner*. It's all *Gott's warrick*, isn't it?" Abram insisted. He was not sure why he was pressing the issue so hard. He had only just met Cerise but he could not shake the feeling that she had been brought here for a reason.

"Maybe…" Matthew agreed dubiously. The men returned to their singing and ended their discussion.

Several times throughout the service, Abram looked up to find Cerise staring at him. They shared smiles until Bishop Speicher called the event to a close.

"Stay for refreshments," the Bishop instructed everyone. "*Chrischdaag* is only a few days away. You may not see your *landsmann* and *freind* before the festive season again so be sure you wish them well."

The men and women rejoined to head toward the refreshment table at the end of the parking lot, the sun fully blazing down to create a slushy, puddling mess for the children to run around and enjoy.

"*Wat* did you think of that?" Abram asked Cerise who smiled broadly and nodded.

"I'm a little underdressed for the occasion I think." She laughed nervously, gesturing at her jeans and sweater. "But it was lovely. Peaceful. Just like Brandy Valley. It's so very different here than the city."

"That's one of the things I found about it too," Joshua agreed, catching the last of her words as he sidled up to them. "I preferred the serenity of the small town to the bustle of Pittsburgh."

Cerise eyed him speculatively. "Don't you miss it?" she asked.

"No," he replied honestly. "Not even at the beginning when I thought it would be the most difficult. *Gott* spoke to me a long time ago and told me that I was supposed to be here. Some people have the calling and *komme*…"

He glanced at Abram who shifted his weight uncomfortably.

"Wait, more people have converted?" Cerise's brow rose in disbelief. Joshua shook his head.

"*Nee*…well, not here. It's happened in other communities but ours is fairly small and new. There have been others who have come here, believing they have what it takes to live among us, but so far, I have been the only one to stay."

Cerise stared at him. "Why?"

Joshua chuckled. "Why what?"

"Why are you the only one?"

"Because it's not so easy. Those who come have a romantic idea of what it is like to live as we do but they don't account for the work involved or the sense of community. Some have the ability to learn the language and *Ordnung* but can't accept the communal responsibility. Others are not so adept at accepting our customs. Everyone is different, Cerise, as you must know in your line of *warrick*."

Cerise nodded slowly and Abram could see the wheels of her bright mind turning.

"*Komme*," Abram interjected, not liking how heavy the conversation was getting. "Let's find you something to *esse, yah*?"

"I'm going to weigh a hundred more pounds by the time I leave here!" She chuckled as he guided her toward the food-laden table.

"*When* you leave here?" he echoed lightly. Cerise paused, her smile fading slightly.

"Abram…I don't know you at all, but I know I like it here. Maybe a bit too much. And I know I like you. You're good for those kids and that goes a long way with me."

Abram waited, his pulse quickening. She sighed heavily. "I don't really know what I'm saying," she muttered. "I guess we should just get through these next few days, shouldn't we? See what happens?"

"Okay," he agreed, trying to keep the disappointment out of his voice.

"Speaking of which..."

"I'm glad you brought that up," Abram said quickly, sparing her the pain of asking. "I've asked Joshua to *komme* for *Chrischdaag nachtesse*—supper—at my *haus*. I trust you'll join us with the *kinner*."

Her eyes brightened happily. "Oh yes, of course! But..."

She bit on her lower lip. "I...am I allowed to get the kids anything for Christmas? Or are presents forbidden? I don't even know..."

Laughing, Abram nodded. "*Yah*, you can get the *kinner* something small. We don't buy many things and tend to make our presents so they're from the heart but obviously, you haven't had the benefit of time on your side for that. Joshua's sister and nephew will join us too—they're English and *komme* every year."

"Oh!" She was stunned by the revelation but Abram was happy to enlighten her.

"We care more about being together and celebrating *Gott* than we do about...things," he explained.

"That's nice. That's what Christmas is supposed to be about, anyway."

"*Yah*, it is. The Amish keep things the way we do so we don't forget the most basic principles of life, *yah*?"

Admiration shone in Cerise's eyes as she nodded, lifting her chin to meet his eyes again.

"I'm looking forward to spending Christmas with your family, Abram. Thank you for including me."

His heart twisted at her sincerity.

She would make the perfect wife, if only she wasn't Englisch.

CHAPTER 5

*C*erise's cell phone remained on silent all day and she had almost forgotten about it until she returned to the car with the children after a lovely dinner with Abram. Their bellies were full and their eyelids drooped as she secured Sadie into her car seat, turning to Abram and promising to visit later in the morning the following day so he'd have more time to prepare for their arrival.

"You can come anytime you like," he said. "In fact, you could stay."

Her cheeks burned at his bold proposal, and she wondered if he was this forward with everyone, but her heart told her that he wasn't.

"Maybe I'll come a little earlier and make breakfast then... mar...mariy—*mariyeesse?*"

Noah snorted from inside the car, but Abram smiled with pride. "You're already getting a handle on *Deutch* after two days! Imagine what a week or month would do!"

"I-I don't know if we'll ever find out," she mumbled.

"I guess that's in *Gott's* hands now, isn't it?" Abram agreed. "If you want to you can *komme* early, but you don't have to make breakfast in the *mariye*—in the morning. I'll try to finish faster."

"There's no need for you to rush. I'm here now. You may as well put me to good use while you have me."

"Maybe you'll find that you like the routine," Abram said with a shrug. "And you'll never want to leave."

Her blush deepened and Cerise was sure she was the shade of a cherry tomato by the time she climbed into her old Buick and headed away from the district, toward the town where their motel was situated.

All the way back, through the deserted country roads, she found her mind slipping to a life where she didn't have to take kids from neglectful parents or rehouse abandoned babies. She imagined a world where an entire community looked out for one another, ensuring that no one was every lonely or poor or forgotten.

It doesn't seem real in the America that I know.

And yet it was real, and right under her nose. A god-fearing group of people who were loving and kind and helpful, who cared about the land and their neighbors.

Why wouldn't I want to stay here?

Abram Hertzler had made it very clear that he would provide for her but how could she ask that of him when she'd just met him? But she also couldn't deny that she had felt a deep attraction to him and to Brandy Valley the moment she had entered the city limits.

She thought of what Joshua had said, about God calling him there, and she wondered if He had called her there too.

A flashing in her purse caught her attention in the darkness of the car and she realized that it was her cell phone going off. She had turned off the Bluetooth connection with the kids in the car as to not disturb them on the trip but she made a mental note to reconnect it.

Oh darn! I bet Muriel's been calling me all day!

She didn't risk answering the call as she drove on the black roads, leading toward the lonely motel off of the highway, but she vowed to call her supervisor as soon as she had the kids settled in for the night.

The neon sign of the Valley Inn Motel appeared, blinking in teal and red. As she parked, the flashing seemed to wake Noah, who was asleep in the front seat.

"Are we here already?" he mumbled, sounding disappointed.

"Yes," Cerise told him, parking the car in front of their joint room. He and his brother shared an adjacent unit to her and Sadie but Cerise left the door wide open so she could keep an eye on all three kids throughout the night. Not that she worried about the boys getting up to trouble but there was a protocol to be followed.

Like I'm not breaking all kinds of protocol by being out here right now, she mused, ushering the kids inside the motel.

"How many more nights do we have to stay here, Cerise?" Noah muttered. The question pierced her chest, his words so sad, so dejected.

"I'm working on getting you to your uncle's place as hard as I can," she promised him. "You have to believe that, Noah. I really am doing everything I can but without my supervisor…"

He grimaced, as if her words were just lies to his ears, but he didn't argue and instead went to help with getting Sadie out of the car.

Sighing, Cerise woke Daniel who stumbled ahead as she instructed both boys to brush their teeth while she readied Sadie for bed.

Ensuring that all the children were tucked away for the night, she took her cell phone and headed out into the frigid night. Without the sunshine, the unseasonable warmth of the day had disappeared, hardening the melting snow to ice again. Cerise watched her step as she found Muriel on her caller list.

"Where the devil have you been all day?" Muriel demanded. "I was about to send a search team out for you!"

Her voice was hoarse and guilt overtook Cerise. "I'm sorry," she answered contritely. "I didn't mean to worry you but I didn't bring my cell with me."

"Why the heck not? You have kids with you! That's a work issued phone! You need to have it on and with you! Always! Are you trying to give me a coronary?!"

"It didn't feel right having my phone there."

"Aw, that's right. The Amish. Don't—" she stopped to cough and concern furrowed Cerise's brow.

"Don't do that again," Muriel concluded. "I really was about to contact the local sheriff."

"Are you all right, Muriel?"

"Who, me? Oh yeah. I've got a bit of a cold or something. Nothing to fret about. I'm powering through it otherwise David will take over things in the office."

"Ugh," Cerise moaned.

"Indeed. Ugh," Muriel agreed, sniffling. She released another cough. "How are things going over there?"

Cerise hesitated, unsure if she should disclose the truth or not.

"Cher?"

"I…it's good. Much better than I expected," she replied slowly. "I mean…much better."

"Oh?" Muriel sounded intrigued.

Encouraged, Cerise went on. "It's so different, you know? I mean, everyone comes together as one. There's no city hustle, no 'me, me, me' attitude. It's a big, huge…"

"Family?" Muriel offered.

"Yes…and they want me to stay."

"Who?!" Muriel's tone switched, a baffled edge taking over. "Who asked you to stay?"

"Abram—the uncle. He's…very kind and great with the kids."

"Oh, I see."

"I don't know, Muriel, I'm really entertaining this. It's apparently been done before and I think I could swing it if I wanted to."

"What's keeping you from doing it?"

Shocked at Muriel's agreeable response, she blinked. "Work, for one," she scoffed.

"Really? Work? You see yourself rehoming broken kids your whole life until you're old and miserable like me? That's your life plan, Cher?"

"You're not..." Cerise started to say but Muriel snorted.

"Don't placate me. I know what I am and what you are. You're empathetic and warm. This job will break you if you let it. Don't let it, Cher."

"I don't know, Muriel. It's something to think about."

Muriel burst into another fit of coughing and Cerise let her off the phone, warning her to take care of herself. "Get some rest. Are you sure you're okay?"

"I'm fine!" Muriel wheezed in the midst of her fit. "Enjoy your Christmas. I'll be in touch but make sure you answer your dang phone."

She hung up and tapped the device to her chin thoughtfully, a warm glow radiating through her body.

At least I know I have Muriel's blessing if I decide to pursue this.

After breakfast, Abram suggested that they all go into town before the shops closed for Christmas Eve.

"Things will close earlier today so it's best we go now," he warned. Noah and Daniel were in agreement but Sadie was quieter than usual.

It was not until they entered the Christmas market that Cerise truly realized that there was something amiss with the little girl, her body language twisting toward the door as Abram caught sight of Joshua and her brothers scampered off to speak with some friends.

"*NEE!*" Sadie shouted suddenly. "*NEE*, I DON'T WANT TO BE HERE!"

Startled by her outburst, Cerise blinked once, staring at the child as if she could not believe the girl had spoken the words.

"Sadie?" she asked slowly. "What's wrong?"

"*NEE!*" she yelled again, stomping her foot. "I want to go *deheem*! I want *Mamm*! I want *Daed*! I don't want to be here!"

Distinctly aware of all the eyes on them, Cerise lowered herself to the child's level and reached out to take her shoulders but Sadie pulled away. "*NEE!*" she sobbed, tears pooling in her eyes. "You're not my *mudder*! You're not!"

"No, I'm not," Cerise agreed softly. "I'm not trying to be your mother, Sadie."

"My *mudder* is gone forever!"

A shadow fell over her and Cerise looked up to see Jacob and Abram standing over her, their confusion as palpable as hers. She shrugged and shook her head.

"Sadie," Cerise tried again, reaching for the child but she backed away even more.

"THEY'RE GONE! *GOTT* TOOK THEM! I HATE HIM!"

Cerise inhaled sharply, knowing that this sentiment probably would not go over well in the religious community, but to her amazement, Joshua knelt down and extended his hand gently toward the child.

"*Nee*, Sadie, your *leit* are not gone forever," he said softly. "Not at all."

"You're lying! They're dead! Danny told me!" she mewled, the tears now sliding down her cheeks.

"*Yah*, it's true that *Gott* has called them to be with Him, but you will see them again when He calls for you, too."

Sadie sniffled and stared at Cerise as if waiting for confirmation. She glanced at Joshua who nodded slightly and Cerise bobbed her head. "It's true, Sadie. I know how you feel too. I lost my parents when I was a baby. I was sad and scared but I'm not anymore because Joshua is right. We will all see each other again."

Abram scooped the little girl up in his arms and wiped her tears away. "In the meantime, you have so many people who love you, *liebling*. So many people who want to feed you *eepie*."

The little girl's face brightened at the mention of cookies and Abram nodded toward a nearby booth as Noah and Daniel joined Cerise's side.

"*Wat* happened?" Noah demanded, watching his tear-streaked sister being led away, Joshua on their heels.

"She's starting to understand that your parents have gone to God now," Cerise replied sadly. Noah cast her a sidelong look.

"Are you going to distract her with a *hochzich*?" he asked, a teasing note to his voice. Daniel chucked but Cerise didn't understand.

"I'm sorry, I don't know that word," she confessed.

"A wedding," Daniel offered. "He's asking if you're going to marry our uncle."

With inflamed cheeks, Cerise gawped at him. "I only just met your uncle!" she breathed, wondering if Abram had put them up to this conversation. But as quickly as the thought had surfaced, she dismissed it. Abram didn't have a sneaky bone in his body. This was the boys detecting something completely on their own, something that maybe even Cerise couldn't see herself yet.

"So what?" Daniel pressed. "You could get to know him better."

"I'm not Amish," she reminded him dryly.

"That can be changed too," Noah added.

They're advocating for me to stay. Is this a sign from God also?

She smiled warmly at the boys and ushered them forward to catch up with their uncle and Joshua.

"Come along, boys. I heard a rumor about cookies up ahead."

She didn't give them an answer because she wasn't sure she had one to give them. She only knew that her heart was battling with her mind...and that her heart seemed to be winning out.

CHAPTER 6

*J*oshua returned to the house with Abram and the children and as Cerise fixed lunch for everyone, the older man took the younger aside.

"She's interested in the community here. She wants to know more," Joshua informed him. "I can see it in her face. I recognize it because she reminds me of myself."

Abram looked at his long-time friend hopefully but with cautious optimism. "What are you saying?" he asked bluntly.

"I'm saying that maybe I should sit and speak with her about what she might need to do if she was serious about staying here."

Abram pursed his lips, his eyes darting toward the living room where his nephews sat with his niece, playing a board game. Dishes clanged about in the kitchen as he considered the minister's words carefully.

"She just got here," Abram mused slowly.

"And she's not apt to be here much longer," Joshua agreed. "Now's the time to bring it to her and let her think it over." He paused. "Unless you don't think it's a good idea."

Abram sighed deeply. "I know that there are a lot of requirements," he admitted. "It's a lot of work."

"Of course it is, otherwise we would just let anyone in here and our purpose would lose its meaning. We have to be selective about our community."

"But it might be overwhelming for her."

"Ah...so what do you propose? Not saying anything and letting her go?"

Abram did not want that either.

"You don't want a *frau* who can't handle the *warrick*," Joshua reminded him and Abram agreed that was true. "Don't underestimate Cerise. She has not had an easy life. I think she craves stability and we can certainly provide that here."

Abram raised his head toward the kitchen, nodding in agreement. "*Yah*, you're right," he conceded. "You should speak to her after lunch. I'll take the *kinner* and tell them what might happen if she agrees to the changes."

"You should prepare them for what happens if she doesn't, also. They seem to have grown quite attached to her. If she leaves, they won't take it well..."

Abram had not even considered that and it poked at his heart to think of the day that Cerise left and never returned.

"I'll talk to them. They've endured enough loss for a lifetime already. It's not fair for them to deal with more."

"I don't think that Cerise would want to hurt them either but if it's not what she wants—"

"I don't want her to be here if she'll be unhappy," Abram interjected quickly. "Let's sort this out."

"Sandwiches?" Cerise called, appearing in the doorway with a tray stacked high.

"Perfect," Abram said, rising to take the plate from her. "Wash your hands, *kinner* and *komme esse*."

The children did as they were told and Joshua turned to Cerise as she moved to sit down at the table. "Cerise, would you come and walk with me?" he asked. Surprised, she glanced up at him, nodding slowly. Casting a look at Abram she picked up a sandwich from the pile and nodded for Joshua to do the same but he refused.

"Lydia is expecting me home soon, but I do want to have a word with you before I go."

"Am I in trouble?" she joked but her cheeks were pale.

"Of course not," Abram called out, offering Joshua a scolding gaze. "I'll be here with the *kinner*."

By the time the children had returned from the bathroom, Cerise and Joshua had bundled into their coats and boots and disappeared into the snow outside, leaving Abram alone at the table.

"Where are Cerise and Joshua?" Noah asked worriedly.

"They'll be back in a little while," Abram promised. "But I wanted a little bit of time with you alone. I haven't had much since you've been here. Is that okay?"

The children nodded, their eyes shining as they took their seats, reaching for a sandwich. "Ooh! Egg salad is my favorite!" Sadie squealed.

"This is why I wanted some time alone with you," Abram explained. "To get to know some of your likes for when you're staying here permanently."

Daniel perked up, cocking his head to the side. "Are we allowed to move in here now?"

"Not yet, but soon," Abram reassured him. "Cerise is working very hard to make that happen but with *Chrischdaag*—"

"Are you going to marry her?" Noah interrupted.

Taken aback by his bluntness, Abram cleared his throat. "Put your sandwiches down, *pliese*. We haven't prayed."

The children obliged guiltily and hung their heads silently with their uncle. After a quiet moment, Abram lifted his head again and allowed them to eat.

"Would you mind if I did marry Cerise?" Abram asked, picking up where they had left off.

"*NEE!*" Sadie screamed predictably as Noah shook his head. Abram fixed his gaze on Daniel who hesitated.

"She's not *Amisch*," he reminded Abram as if the man could have forgotten.

"She may be willing to take the steps to join the community."

"Is it that easy?" Daniel asked sourly.

"*Nee*. It's not easy at all," Abram countered. "It's very difficult, in fact. She needs to learn the *Ordnung*, become fluent in *Deutch*, learn all our customs and ways. She will need the support of the community—there are many things she'll have to do before she's considered."

Daniel's face softened slightly. "And she would do all that?"

"Maybe."

"She would if she wants to marry you," Noah insisted.

"They have to court first, *schtupid*," Sadie chimed in.

"Don't call your *bruder schtupid*," Abram scolded her. Sadie stared at him with huge, green eyes.

"Then he shouldn't be *schtupid*," she insisted and Abram swallowed a laugh.

"Sadie…"

"You'll get married right away," Sadie announced, popping a bit of sandwich into her mouth. "And I'll be at the wedding…"

"I think you're getting a little ahead of yourself." Abram snickered but he could not help but feel excited by their infectious enthusiasm.

They want her here too.

"But if she chooses not to stay, you will have to learn to accept that as well," Abram warned them. "Her life was never here in the first place."

"She'll stay," Noah said with all the conviction of an eleven-year-old. "She loves you."

Heat rose into Abram's cheeks and he peered at his brother's son, realizing how much the boy reminded him of Elijah.

Oh how I miss you, Abram thought mournfully, the bittersweetness of life twisting his stomach. He had lost his brother but gained Elijah's sons. With or without a wife, he would provide the best life possible for them but he truly hoped that Cerise would stay.

"I don't want you to get your hopes up or make her feel guilty if she decides to return to the city," Abram insisted, secretly praying that Noah was right. "Do you promise me to let Cerise make her own decisions?"

The boys nodded but Sadie was no longer listening as she played with her food.

"*Gut.* Now, let's talk about what needs to be done for *mariye.* It's *Chrischdaag*…did you know that?"

The children grinned but Abram could read the sadness in their eyes. It would be the first one without their parents and he could never replace them, no matter how hard he tried.

But I will always do my best for them and by them.

The front door opened and everyone turned to watch the freezing pair pour back into the house, stomping their feet and rubbing their hands.

"Noah, go throw another log on the fire," Abram asked, and Noah scampered off to obey.

He stared at the entranceway as Cerise looked at his gaze, a serene smile touching her lips. The smile set his heart racing and he realized that she had made her decision.

If all goes well, by next Chrischdaag, Cerise will be my wife.

CHAPTER 7

*C*erise's head spun in the aftermath of the discussion with Joshua.

Am I really considering this? Could I live here, among the Amish?

It was incredible to think that a few days ago, Cerise had known nothing about these people, mistaking them for the Mennonites, and now...

Now what?

The stroll she had taken with Joshua had begun innocently enough but Cerise had understood why the minister had taken her away from the children and Abram.

Now, as she sat in the living room, surrounded by their chatter, she found herself replaying Joshua's words.

"If you're really entertaining this idea, there are some hard truths you'll need to know about living among the *Amisch*," Joshua had said. "This order is more liberal than some but we still don't use electricity, as you may have gleaned. You would have to give up your car, your cell phone...your hair dryer."

Joshua's eyes gleamed with amusement as Cerise scoffed.

"But it's more than just the physical change that you will have to overcome. It's the spiritual one. You will have to learn our language better than *Englisch*. It's akin to *Englisch* in a lot of ways, however. *Englisch* is a Germanic language."

"Cerise!"

She blinked and realized that everyone was staring at her. Embarrassed, she returned their gazes. "What?"

"You haven't said a word all afternoon," Abram commented gently, casting Noah a reproving glance for his barking. "Are you all right?"

"Of course!" She laughed nervously. "I'm just thinking."

"About marrying Abram?" Sadie chirped. Cerise's cheeks set on fire at the question as Daniel chortled.

"Have you given any thought to staying?" Noah pressed but Abram put an end to the line of questions.

"It's *Chrischdaag* Eve," he said firmly. "It's a time for togetherness and prayer, not peppering our guest with questions."

"Just one more," Noah begged. "Have you heard anything about us staying here *dienacht*? I don't want to spend *Chrischdaag* at the motel."

Sympathy rushed through Cerise in a torrent but she shook her head. "I'm sorry, Noah," she murmured. "We still have to go back there tonight."

Daniel groaned as Sadie whimpered but Abram shook his head. "That's fine. You'll *komme* back in the *mariye, yah*? It's better that way."

All three children stared at him dubiously but Abram was quick to add his explanation.

"I have more time to prepare for *Chrischdaag mariye*," he said, glancing at Joshua who nodded.

"Next year, and every year afterward, you'll be here," the minister offered. "This year, things are a little more complicated but you have Cerise to help navigate you through."

"*Denki Gott* for that," Noah muttered. Cerise was unsure if the boy was being sarcastic or not but when she met his sad, green eyes, she realized he was serious. Her heart ached for all of them, orphaned and uprooted so close to Christmas, unable to sleep in their own beds.

I get it, kids. I've been here myself. Except I never had a home to go to...until now.

"I'll make dinner," Cerise suggested. "And then we'll make it an early night. We wouldn't want to interrupt Santa."

The children snorted.

"There's no Santa, Cerise," Sadie told her, matter-of-factly and Cerise stifled a sigh. She still had a great deal to learn about the Amish way of life.

For the first time, the children were not sleepy on the way back to the motel, the Christmas spirit fully infecting them.

"I wish we could have stayed there *dienacht*," Daniel reiterated, and Cerise glanced at him in the rear-view mirror.

"I'm sure that you'll be there soon," she offered weakly, knowing that she had been saying the same thing over and over for days.

"I wish *Mamm* and *Daed* were here," Sadie moaned. Cerise sensed a long night ahead but as she glanced at Noah he looked back at her from the passenger seat.

"I'm grateful that we got you to take care of us, Cerise," he told her earnestly. Her chest tightened.

"You would have been in *gut* hands no matter what," she promised.

Noah chortled with glee. "You keep speaking in *Deutch*!" he observed. "You really are thinking about staying, aren't you?"

Cerise swallowed the lump in her throat and stared out into the black night, unsure of how to answer his question. Every hour that passed in Abram's living room, she realized that she was falling in love with the kind and patient man who had opened his house and heart to his nephews and niece without complaint.

But could she truly give up her whole life and start over in a place so different?

What life? What do I have that's keeping me in Philly?

"You don't have to answer," Noah told her with far more wisdom than an eleven-year-old should possess. "I can see it in your eyes."

The motel was alive with Christmas music and a party happened a few doors down. A rowdy couple waved a hand and invited them over for eggnog, reminding Cerise of how she had ended up there in the first place.

"Go brush your teeth," she instructed the children. "I'm going to call my boss."

The Hertzler kids moved to their respective bathrooms to do as Cerise requested and she located her cell phone. To her surprise, there were no missed calls from Muriel and when she tried to call her supervisor, the call went directly to voicemail.

"Hey, it's just Cerise checking in. I guess there's no update on the Hertzler kids. Well…Merry Christmas. I'll touch base with you on Boxing Day. I hope you're feeling better."

She hung up after leaving the message and sighed, retreating to the room she was sharing with Sadie.

"Hey! Lady!" the drunk woman from room 124 yelled out to her, and Cerise had half a mind to ignore her.

"You the mom of all those kids?"

"The aunt," Cerise answered without thinking. Her cheeks pinkened at the lie but she didn't correct herself, it was simply easier to tell the woman what she wanted to hear.

"Well aren't you going to have a fun Christmas!" the woman chortled. "You sure you don't want to come over? Wait for them to fall asleep and come have a nip or two. My Brian makes the best rum punch!"

"No thanks," Cerise replied, her hand on the knob. "I'm exactly where I want and need to be."

She let herself into the room and locked it behind her, peering at Sadie's already sleeping face on the pillow of the single twin bed. The exhaustion of the day had already caught up with her.

Quietly, she crept toward the open door of the adjacent room and looked toward the other twin beds, noting that both boys had crawled onto their mattresses also. They hadn't seen her there but they were still awake, whispering amongst themselves.

"...she'll stay?" Daniel mumbled, his voice thick with sleep.

"I think she wants to stay but it's not an easy choice to make."

"She doesn't have a *familye* to go *deheem* to," Daniel insisted. "Why doesn't she stay here with us?"

They're talking about me.

"It's in *Gott's* hands now, Danny. There's *nix* we can do but pray that Cerise won't leave us too." Noah sighed. His words pierced Cerise's soul and she backed away, tears filling her eyes.

They would get over me leaving. They're only depending on me now because they have to stay with me...aren't they?

Ensuring that Sadie was soundly asleep, Cerise released her hair from the messy bun and her long hair spilled over her shoulders as she changed into a pair of plaid, flannel pajamas. Then, she knelt by the bed and closed her eyes, bowing her head.

Dear God, she prayed silently. *Please guide me on what to do here. I can't decide what the right choice is. My heart is pulling me in the direction of Abram and the children but is it too much, too soon? Please, give me a sign?*

Her eyes opened and she again glanced over at the sleeping child before crawling into her own bed and turning out the light.

God is busy. It's Christmas Eve. He's got bigger fish to fry tonight than me.

~

"Cerise! Cerise, wake up! It's *Chrischdaag*! It's *Chrischdaag*, Cerise!"

Blinking the sleep away, the young woman opened her eyes to find Sadie smiling over her, the palest dawn light pouring through the motel windows as her brothers stood awkwardly behind her.

"*Es dutt mer leed*," Daniel mumbled, embarrassed. "We told her to let you sleep."

"It's all right," Cerise replied with a little laugh, shoving the covers away from her body. "It's Christmas. No one should sleep in on Christmas."

She realized that all three children were already dressed and ready to go, hurrying her along to do the same. "Give me ten minutes, okay?"

"Okay!" they chorused excitedly.

Stifling a yawn, Cerise made her way into the bathroom and splashed cold water on her face to wash away the remnants of sleep.

She stared at herself in the foggy mirror of the motel bathroom as she pinned her hair on top of her head.

It should feel weird spending Christmas with a bunch of strangers but it doesn't. Because they don't feel like strangers to me. They feel like my family.

Grinning to herself, she hastily dressed in the clothes she had already laid out the night before and headed out to meet the children who sat patiently by the door.

Cerise tossed the keys to Noah. "I'll meet you at the car in a minute. I just need to grab some things."

Noah and Daniel exchanged a baffled look and Cerise chuckled, showing them how to unlock the doors with the key fob.

"Put Sadie in her car seat. I'll be right out."

They headed out without complaint and she hurried toward the closet where she had hidden their gifts. Slipping into her boots and jacket, she retreated from the room to meet the kids at the car, popping the trunk to put all the presents in the back.

If the children had noticed her arms full of packages, they made no comment and they were off, winding up the road against a very light snow.

"Do you mind if I put on the radio?" Cerise asked them. "For a little bit of Christmas music?"

The children shifted uncomfortably in their seats and Cerise realized that they weren't supposed to listen to secular music.

"Or…" she suggested. "You could sing for me. What about some of the hymns I heard the other day? Do you know them?"

Immediately, Sadie's sweet voice filled the car and Cerise smiled, navigating the ride as her brothers joined in. The melody of their song transported Cerise out of the car and into the white landscape, along the snow toward the glow of the sun which rose over the white-capped pines.

By the time they arrived at Abram's house, Cerise's heart was so full, she had not realized that tears of joy had flooded her eyes.

"Are you all right?" Abram asked, meeting them at the car.

"Happy *Chrischdaag, Onkle!*" Sadie cried, throwing her arms around him and sparing Cerise from explaining her emotional state. She was unsure she would have been able to put it into words. The elation inside her was unlike anything she had ever experienced before.

"Happy *Chrischdaag, liebling,*" Abram said, scooping her up to keep her tiny feet from kicking up the freshly fallen snow. He cast Cerise a curious look but she shook her head.

"It's fine," she reassured him. "I'm fine."

"*Komme* inside," Abram urged everyone. "Joshua is already here with his *schweschder* and her *sohn.*"

Nervously, Cerise moved to the trunk to get her gifts and Abram handed Sadie to Noah, lingering back to help.

"Are you sure you're all right?" he asked worriedly. "Were they giving you trouble?"

"No! No, not at all!" She paused. "They were singing to me."

Impressed, Abram chuckled. "Oh. I don't think I've ever heard the three of them singing together. Maybe I should ask them to do that later."

"Please don't," Cerise begged. "It was so beautiful and I wouldn't want them to think I was..."

She shrugged. "I don't want to ruin it."

"They've taken a real shining to you, *yah?*" Abram commented. Cerise thought of what she had overheard the night before and bit on her lower lip, grabbing the last of the packages and closing the trunk solidly.

"I'm the only constant they've had since their parents..." she hesitated, realizing that this was Abram's brother she was speaking about. "Your brother and sister-in-law have passed. It's natural that they've clung to me."

"It's more than that, Cerise," Abram told her tenderly, placing a hand on her arm before she could take another step. "They see the same thing in you that I do, that Joshua does. You're *gut*, decent. There had to be other options than you *cooma* all the way out here from the city to let the *kinner* spend *Chrischdaag* with me."

Cerise started to shake her head but Abram wasn't having it. "You couldn't have stayed in the city?"

"Well...yes..."

"But you didn't. You chose to bring the *kinner* here so they could be close to their *familye*. And even if you didn't have your own *familye*, I'm sure you had other plans, didn't you?"

She thought of the ticket to Aspen where Madison was off skiing right then, but somehow, Cerise wasn't jealous. She couldn't think of a lonelier place to be than where her co-worker had ended up.

"I'm right about you and so are the *kinner*. *Gott* sent you here, to us."

"Are you going to stand out here all day?" Joshua called out from the porch. "The *kinner* are eying their gifts and Mason has been waiting patiently to open his all *mariye!*"

Abram dropped his arm and Cerise swallowed her disappointment. "Mason?" she repeated, following him up the slippery pathway toward the house.

"Joshua's *neffyu*," Abram explained. "His *schweschder* is here, remember?"

"Right. The *Englischers*."

Abram grinned at her and nodded, shooing her and Joshua inside, the smell of turkey already cooking in the oven. Cerise turned to look at the sun glinting off the snow like tiny sparkling diamonds, a few cattle roaming through the fields, their earmuffs on for warmth. She laughed at the sight and moved to take a photo but realized she had left her phone at the motel.

It doesn't matter. It doesn't belong here anyway. I won't forget any of this.

~

Mary-Beth was surprisingly warm although Cerise didn't know why she was surprised by this fact. She had expected Joshua's sister to be sterner and more disapproving of her brother's life choices than she was.

"Doesn't it bother you that he's *Amisch* now?" Cerise whispered after they had finished supper and the women washed dishes while a cherry pie baked in the oven for dessert.

"Why would it?" Mary-Beth asked curiously.

"I don't know...I mean, he's not living in the city..."

She laughed and cocked her head. "But I can visit him any time I like," she replied. "Like right now."

"Oh..." Cerise felt silly that she had asked but Mary-Beth chuckled again.

"I know. I had a lot of questions too when Joshua told me that he wanted to convert—a lot of misconceptions. But he's so content here, Cerise, and truly, I'm happy for him."

She nodded as Joshua's sister returned to her son and brother, leaving Cerise to deal with her homemade pie. It had been years since she had attempted to make one from scratch and she hoped it would come out all right.

"It smells so *gut*!" Noah complained, ambling into the kitchen with his new scarf wrapped around his neck. Cerise smiled to see him wearing the gift she had carefully picked out for him. "Is it ready yet?"

"Almost," she promised. "A couple of more minutes."

"There's fresh cream for that outside," Abram announced, joining them in the room.

"Is the pie ready yet?" Daniel wanted to know as Sadie trailed after him.

"Pie? I like pie! Almost as much as *eepie*!"

Giggling, Cerise removed the dessert from the oven as the children gathered around to inhale in deeply.

"That's beautiful!" Abram declared. "Where did you learn how to bake like that?"

"I don't know," Cerise admitted. "I taught myself."

"Can we eat it?" Sadie demanded.

"Let it cool first," Cerise ordered, ushering them back into the living room. To her astonishment, there were a small pile of plainly wrapped gifts in the middle of the living room.

"Oh...someone didn't open their presents," she announced, looking around in confusion. She hadn't seen them before.

"They're yours," Abram declared gleefully, glancing at the children whose smiles matched him. Cerise blushed and shook her head.

"No..." she mumbled. "You didn't have to do that..."

"Of course, we didn't have to," Abram agreed, encouraging her to sit and open her presents. "That's not what *Chrischdaag* is about. We did it because we wanted to."

"You've become very special to us, Cerise," Noah added softly as she sat, her eyes shining in wonderment.

"And we hope you decide to stay," Daniel blurted out.

"Forever!" Sadie added. "Not just until we move here."

Cerise pressed her lips together to keep her chin from quivering as she looked from one face to the next, Joshua nodding as he stood behind the wing chair where his sister sat with a broad smile on her face.

They always knew I was going to stay. They knew before I did, she thought, tears blurring her eyes again.

"Hurry up and open your *yetzich*!" Sadie ordered her. "I want pie!"

Cerise changed into the simple, but pretty, homespun dress of blue before she left Abram's house with the children. Sarah Byler had made it herself, Abram claimed, along with the woollen mittens and scarf that Noah and Daniel presented to her.

Sadie had already fallen asleep and Abram carried her to the car, careful not to slide in the snow over the driveway before setting her in the backseat with her half-sleeping brothers.

"*Denki* for a beautiful *Chrischdaag*," Cerise told Abram nervously, distinctly aware of Joshua and Mary-Beth watching them from the porch. She was sure that if they had not been there, Abram might try to steal a kiss, even with his nephews there.

Or maybe that's just a fantasy I made up.

"Will I see you tomorrow?" Abram asked huskily.

"Of course." Cerise giggled. "That's why I'm here. To bring the kids to you."

He reached up to brush a strand of hair from her face and she blushed furiously, bowing her head.

Maybe it's a good thing he didn't try to kiss me. My head is ready to pop off as it is.

"It's not just the *kinner* that I want to see," he told her affectionately. "I thought you would have figured that out by now."

Cerise peered up at him through her lashes and nodded. "I'll be here tomorrow," she promised and he opened the driver's side for her, allowing her into the car. Both the boys had fallen asleep already.

It was all Cerise could do to keep from humming to herself all the way back to the motel, her mood better than she could ever remember it being.

"Boys," she whispered when they arrived at the Valley Inn Motel. "We're here."

Noah's eyes fluttered sleepily but he nudged Daniel and together, they climbed wordlessly out of the car as Cerise lifted Sadie from the back seat.

The boys stumbled to their room, mumbling good-nights, but Cerise didn't fault them for their lack of communication. It had been a long, full day and she had no doubt that they would sleep in tomorrow.

Removing Sadie's shoes, she tucked the little girl into her bed and dressed in her pajamas, remembering her cell phone just as she was about to crawl into bed herself.

The device blinked where it was charging and Cerise hurried toward it, realizing that she must have missed a call from Muriel.

But when she looked at the screen, her complexion waned. There were six missed calls—none of them from Muriel.

David?!

Drawing in a breath, Cerise called her voicemail, the pleasure of the day fading away as David's strained voice piped through the speaker.

"Cerise, you have a company phone for a reason. Please answer it when I call," the first message intoned. The second message was much less pleasant.

"Cerise, you have children of the state in your care. You will answer to your superior when he calls! Call me back as soon as you get this!"

The third message was borderline abusive.

"So help me God, Cerise, I will come down to Amish Hicksville and grab you myself if you don't start answering me. I don't give a damn that it's Christmas. Call me back or else!"

With shaking hands, Cerise put the phone down and stared at her sleeping charges, unsure of what to do.

Where is Muriel? Why is David calling in her place?

And as she stood there, deciding what to do next, the phone rang in her hand.

CHAPTER 8

The sound of the car's tires on the snow hurried Abram out to the porch with a smile on his face. Wafts of grits and bacon followed him into the cold as he waved toward his family but when the car stopped, he was not immediately overrun by his niece and nephews.

Inexplicably, a feeling of dread prickled down his spine as he made his way down the salted steps toward the car and the driver's side door opened.

"...a minute to explain, Noah!" Cerise was saying harshly. Her tone was sharper than he had ever heard it.

"What's wrong?" Abram asked, his smile fading entirely.

"I don't want to go!" Sadie screamed from the backseat, struggling against her car seat. "I don't want to!"

Dumbfounded, Abram stared at Cerise as she climbed out but before she could utter a word, Noah and Daniel fled the vehicle and raced toward the house.

"Boys, don't do this!" Cerise cried, smacking her hand against her face. "If you don't come…"

"Cerise! What is going on?" Abram frowned, panic settling in. "What happened?"

She bit on her lower lip as if she were about to start crying. "I'm sorry," she whispered. "There's nothing I can do about it."

"About what? What happened?" he implored her. "Why is everyone so upset?"

"She's going to take us away!" Sadie wailed. "She's going to give us away!"

"No, *liebling*, no!" Cerise moaned. "I-I'm not. It's not my choice…"

"Cerise, what is she talking about?"

The door to the house opened and Joshua emerged with Mary-Beth behind him. "What is going on out here?" the minister queried. Mary-Beth rubbed her hands against her arms, shaking her graying head in confusion.

"My supervisor…he wants me to bring the kids back to the city," Cerise rasped.

"He?" Abram was perplexed. "I thought your supervisor was a woman?"

"She is—she was…" Cerise paused and took a breath, leaning against the car door, the wind clearly knocked out of her. "She was getting sick the last time I spoke to her and she warned me that David might take over. He's…he's not a happy person. He makes it his life's quest to make everyone else miserable too."

"I don't understand," Abram muttered. "Come inside. It's *kald* out here—"

"I can't come inside, Abram. I have to take the kids back to the city. A placement just opened up at a youth shelter for them—and at a foster home for Sadie."

Stunned, Abram recoiled. "You would separate them?"

"I'm not doing this!" Cerise cried mournfully. "I told him that they have family, that you're their uncle but he says without proof of relationship, he can't give the kids to you."

"Proof of…what does he want? What does he need?"

"Birth certificates…identification…"

"Does he know we're *Amisch*?" Abram demanded, his face growing hot.

"Yes…" She dropped her chin to avoid his gaze. "I think that's why he's doing this."

Cerise's cell phone began to ring through her car's speakers and she looked helplessly at him. "It's David."

"Answer it," he told her. "I'll speak with him."

Through his peripheral vision, he saw Joshua and Mary-Beth amble down the stairs, neither of them affected by the cold any longer.

"Are you on your way?" David cried when Cerise answered.

"No…I'm at the children's uncle's house."

"Those aren't the instructions I gave you!" the man snapped. "I don't know what's going on or who approved you going out there in the first place but rest assured, I will write you up for this, Cerise."

"This is Abram Hertzler. I'm the paternal uncle of the children.

"I DON'T WANT TO GO!" Sadie howled. Abram turned to Cerise who nodded and unclipped the little girl from her seat, carrying her toward the house.

"I don't know if you are who you say you are, sir," David retorted. "You people don't have any proper paperwork. You could be anyone. If you can prove who you claim to be, then bring your proof to the courthouse and we'll see about granting you custody. Until then..."

Cerise returned. "David, be reasonable. Don't you think the boys would know their own uncle?"

"I don't depend on the affirmations of prepubescent children as legal confirmation. Moreover, I'm not sure I'm comfortable releasing three minors to the care of a single man."

Mouth agape, Cerise stared at the dashboard of her car. "That's not your decision to make! You can't—"

"You don't tell me how to do my job, Ms. Armitage. You're lucky I don't send a police escort down there, but if you're not on the road in the next ten minutes, that's exactly what I'm going to do. Do I make myself clear?"

Cerise's lower lip trembled. "Y-yes."

The phone disconnected and she looked helplessly at Abram. "I don't know what to do!" she wept, shaking her head. "He will send the police, and legally, I have no choice."

She sniffed and straightened her spine. "As soon as Muriel gets back, she'll straighten this out and I'll speak to whomever I have to when I'm back in the city," she vowed. "I won't let them stay there long."

"You need a good lawyer, Abram," Mary-Beth chimed in. "That's what we'll do."

"*Nee!*" Joshua and Abram chorused.

"No lawyers. We don't need to end up facing the legal system," Abram added. "That's not what we need."

"What then?" Mary-Beth asked, frustrated. "They can't just take the kids like that! They're always complaining about how overcrowded the system is and when there's loving family willing to step up…"

"It's okay, Mary-Beth," her brother told her softly. "*Gott* won't let the *kinner* get far. We'll figure something out."

Silent tears streamed down Cerise's face. "I have to take them, Abram. I-I'm so sorry."

"It's not your fault," he told her gently. "You've done everything you could for them."

"Go get them, Josh, *pliese*," Abram informed the minister. The older siblings turned toward the house to collect the Hertzler children as Abram and Cerise stared at one another for a long moment.

"I won't rest until I get them back," she promised, her voice choked.

"Neither of us will," he promised. "Because I'm *cooma* with you."

Startled, Cerise stared at him. "What?!"

"I'm coming with you to the city. You're not going to face this alone, Cerise. The *kinner* are my responsibility."

"We're *cooma* too," Joshua added, joining them with Noah and Daniel at his side. The boys looked up hopefully.

"In fact, I'm going to call on all the *landsmann* and the Bishop too," Joshua went on, fire flaming in his eyes. "The whole district is *cooma* to Philadelphia and we're not *cooma* back until we have the *kinner deheem* with us again."

Sadie still sobbed, not understanding as Abram hurried back to put on his coat and boots.

What if I don't get the kinner back? he wondered, his heart in his throat. *What then?*

He closed his eyes and prayed to God, one hand on the doorknob.

Pliese, Gott, they've all been through enough already. Don't give them any more challenges. They don't deserve it.

Opening his eyes, he squared his shoulders and plastered on a look of confidence that he did not feel. He hoped that God would hear him and keep his nephews and niece safe.

CHAPTER 9

There was no parking when Cerise arrived at the Children's Aid parking lot, almost three hours later, with the children and Abram. There had been several stops along the way, Sadie insisting many times that she had to use the washroom but Cerise knew that she and her brothers were just prolonging the inevitable.

David is going to have kittens when I get in there, she thought miserably, parking in the lot across the street, but she couldn't get over the overflowing parking lot as they walked through.

"That's odd," she muttered, confused by the sight of all the cars. "Hardly anyone should be here today. It's not even this full when we're all here."

"That's Mary-Beth's car," Abram pointed out and Cerise saw that he was right.

"Is this where we're going to live now?" Daniel asked, his face puckered into a frown.

"No...no, this is the CAS building," Cerise explained quietly, leading the way into the offices. "I...I'll have to leave you here and David will have you taken to your placement homes."

She couldn't imagine a world where he allowed her to take them herself. Another lump formed in her throat but as she opened the inner door, pure chaos broke out.

A din like she'd never heard erupted in her ears as David yelled over the sound of dozens of voices. It took Cerise a few seconds to understand what was happening, her gaze widening to take in the flock of Amish men and women flooding the Children's Aid offices. She could barely see through the thick of the familiar faces, their straw hats mixing with white and black prayer bonnets as they accosted David.

"I need you all to leave!" David shouted. "You can't be here!"

"You can't take *kinner* from their *familye*!" someone called out.

"During *Chrischdaag*, no less!" someone else agreed.

David's eyes narrowed and he reached for his landline threateningly. "You are trespassing on government property!" he growled. "I'll have you forcibly removed if you don't leave now!"

"They're not trespassing, David," Cerise interjected, brushing her way through the throng. "They're here at the behest of the Hertzler children. Their community is here to show their support."

The din of voices died down as Cerise spoke, the district from Brandy Valley stepping back to allow Cerise through. Some smiled encouragingly.

David replaced the receiver on the cradle and glowered at her. "You! You orchestrated this!"

"Orchestrated what? Community support? That's a little dramatic, isn't it?" she snorted. "They're here on behalf of the siblings. They want the kids home, where they belong."

"Get them out!" David yelled, stomping his foot. "Get them out now!"

"They have every right to be here and advocate for the children. They're not being violent or disruptive. They've traveled almost two hours, all these families, during their holidays, to advocate for these orphaned kids who only have their community."

David was unmoved, Cerise's words only incensing him more. "This isn't the way it's done and you know it! This is unprofessional and the higher ups are going to hear all about this little stunt!"

Cerise felt anger rise to her cheeks but she remembered whose company she kept and steeled herself from stooping to David's level.

"About me and my stunt?" she echoed. "Is that the stance you're taking?"

He sneered at her. "I'll have your job for this. This is all on camera, Ms. Armitage."

"Chapter 45, part 1355.25 section E in the Principals of Child and Family Service Act reads: Services are timely, flexible, coordinated, and accessible to families and individuals, principally delivered in the home or the community, and are delivered in a manner that is respectful of and builds on the strengths of the community and cultural groups."

She paused and stared straight at David. "Delivered in a manner that is respectful and builds on the strength of the community and cultural groups."

"That doesn't apply here!" David hollered, slamming his fists against the desk.

"Because you pick and choose what applies to you?" Cerise pushed back. "The entire community is literally right here. The children's uncle is right here."

She turned and gestured toward Abram who stepped forward, nodding vigorously. "He's willing to take them. There's absolutely no justifiable reason to send the boys to a shelter and separate the little girl from her brothers."

"There is if I say there is!" David shrieked. "I'm going to see you fired!"

"Tsk, tsk, David. Have you forgotten that this is all on camera?" Cerise asked sweetly. "In fact, I bet that Muriel has access to the recordings directly from home. Let me give her a call and see how she feels about the way you're acting right now."

Cerise reached into her bag for her cell phone as David sputtered.

"Wait! Stop!" he cried but Cerise didn't put the phone down. "I SAID STOP!"

"Cerise..." Abram's tone was rife with worry and Cerise lowered the phone but kept it close.

"Be reasonable. These people have no paperwork, Cerise," David told her coldly. "I'm looking out for the kids."

"*These people?*" she echoed tersely. "*These people* have more sense of loyalty, compassion and unity than you'll ever know in your life."

"I knew it! You're totally unprofessional. You got over-invested with these weirdos, didn't you? I'll have your job for this!"

"Ha!" Cerise snorted. "Good luck with that. I'm quitting anyway."

David gaped at her.

"What?"

"Why would I ever want to work in a place that puts men like you in charge?" she asked, throwing her hands up. "A man who would gleefully and smugly rip kids away from the only family they have—during Christmas, too! You're supposed to be protecting children, David. Instead, you're acting like some Grinch on steroids. Honestly, I want no part of this."

"I'm not—"

"You're not what? Creating extra expense for the City of Philadelphia by putting three kids in the system that actually have a family? I'm sure that will go over well with the powers that be," Cerise added. "Because you know how much the city loves to throw away money."

She threw her head up and met his eyes evenly.

"I'm not..." David started again weakly but trailed off, blood draining from his face entirely. Cerise held her breath, silently praying that he could not see how desperately she hoped her words were affecting him.

"I'll explain everything in my final report," Cerise concluded when David said nothing. "But as you said, the video footage will speak for itself. Come on, everyone. We should let David do his job of separating orphans."

She spun purposefully on her heel as Sadie cried out.

"NO!" the girl wailed and Cerise closed her eyes.

"Wait!"

She stopped and drew in a breath, catching Abram's confused eyes as she turned back. "What now?"

"I-I'll sign off on the uncle," he muttered. "But you can't fill out a report."

Cerise's insides quivered.

"Sign first," she told him grimly. "Then I'll see how I'm feeling."

David glared at her but Cerise held her ground. "Hurry up. We've all been traveling for hours. We're hungry and tired."

Muttering to himself, David sat at his desk and started the paperwork. "Get these people out of here."

"They'll leave when Abram's signature is on the temporary custody form," Cerise shot back. "Make it a month long injunction. That should give Muriel enough time to be back and recovered."

David said nothing as he flicked his eyes back toward the computer screen but his jaw twitched furiously.

"What's going on?" Abram whispered but Cerise held up a hand and shook her head. She didn't want to give him false hope, in case the unpredictable David changed his mind at the last minute.

"Is he getting the *kinner*?" Joshua asked.

"She's working on it, Josh," Mary-Beth told him as Cerise leaned down to pick up Sadie.

"I don't like him," Sadie whispered in her ear.

"Me neither," Cerise agreed, bouncing the girl in her arms as Abram stepped closer to her protectively. Several minutes passed as David continued to type, his frown growing deeper until finally, the printer started to print.

Cerise handed the little girl to her uncle and grabbed the pages from the printer, reaching for a pen off David's desk.

"Sign it," she ordered him, tapping at the line. Without a word, he did what she asked and Cerise had Abram do the same.

"It's done," she announced to the crowd. "We can all go home now."

"You haven't heard the end of this, Cerise," David growled from behind her.

"Oh, but I have," Cerise reassured him, marching toward the door with the others behind her. "Because I'm never coming back here. Not ever."

She didn't turn around to see his reaction but she could feel his disbelief following her out of the offices as the district scattered toward the respective cars.

"Where did everyone get cars from?" Cerise laughed, nodding at the vehicles that had overtaken the parking lot. It was only then that she noticed how many English were in the crowd, all of them doing the driving.

"The *Amisch* have friends everywhere," Abram chuckled, placing Sadie on the slushy sidewalk, next to her brothers.

"I can see that!" Cerise said admiringly. "And *denki Gott* for that!"

"Boys, take Sadie to the car," Abram asked his nephews kindly. They nodded, their eyes shining as they grinned at Cerise.

"We'll be right there," Cerise promised, handing them her keys.

They made their way across the busy street, startled by the city traffic, but once they were safely across, Abram turned Cerise around, his hands on her shoulders.

"*Denki* for what you did."

"It shouldn't have taken all of us coming down here to do that." Cerise sighed, shaking her head ruefully. "What a jerk."

She was distinctly aware of Abram's hands on her shoulders and she tipped her head back to look at him.

"Did you mean what you said?" he asked quietly. The noise of the street around them dulled as Cerise stared deeply into his warm eyes.

"About what?"

"About not *cooma* back here?"

Cerise gulped and nodded. "I-I don't think I could do this again," she replied. "My social working days are done."

"What *will* you do?" Abram asked softly, moving slightly closer to her, a hand brushing sweetly against her cheek.

"I don't know," she replied shyly. "There's this cute little town I know, just a little bit southwest of here. It's called Brandy Valley and it's filled with the most lovely, honest, caring people."

"Really?" Abram teased.

"It's so peaceful and the people are kind, loving, generous and accepting—even of newcomers."

Abram nodded, making a small pout of his lips as if he was considering her words very carefully.

"That sounds like a good place. It's a wonder you didn't move there before."

"It is a good place, and if I'd known before I probably would have."

Abram's smile broadened. "And you want to know what the best thing about that place is?" Cerise murmured, her breath warm against Abram's cheek.

"What's that?"

"You."

Their lips brushed gently against one another and one of the English friends honked their horn playfully on the way out of the parking lot, driving the pair apart.

"*Komme.*" Abram laughed, taking her hand. "Let's go *deheem.*"

"*Yah,*" Cerise agreed. "Let's go home."

EPILOGUE

ONE YEAR LATER

$\mathcal{N}$oah and Daniel stared around the empty schoolroom in dismay, their eyebrows raised in a comical and identical fashion.

"We're supposed to clear all the desks?" Daniel asked, disheartened.

"You did volunteer to *hilf*," Cerise reminded him dryly.

"You're so *glick* you get to be in the pageant," Sadie moaned, pouting lightly from her spot at the back of the schoolhouse.

"One more year, *liebling*, and you'll be a part of it too," Cerise reminded her for the hundredth time. "Where is your *onkle*?"

"He went to get all the supplies you asked for," Daniel said. "Although I don't know why you need so much stuff!"

Cerise blushed and shrugged. "I want to make sure that it's perfect," she admitted. "It's my first year running the pageant. If something goes wrong…"

"*Nix* is going to go wrong," Abram announced, bustling through the door with a crate in his arms. "Sarah Byler says she'll be over after she closes the store to *hilf* you."

"Oh I wish you hadn't asked her, Abram!" Cerise groaned but he waved dismissively after placing the box on one of the desks.

"You worry too much still what everyone thinks of you. Everyone here has accepted you—even before you were baptized and became a *lehrer* for their *kinner*. They liked you when you were a boring, *auld Englisch frau*."

"*Auld*!" Cerise feigned anger and the children laughed.

"We're still the oldest courting couple in Brandy Valley," Abram said and Cerise rolled her eyes skyward.

"Well, there's not much I can do about that," she informed him. The boys cast their uncle a sidelong look and he turned away quickly—but not before Cerise caught the grin between them.

"*Wat* was that?" she demanded.

"*Wat?*" Noah asked.

"*Nix*," Daniel fibbed.

"I'm going back to the *haus*. You're *cooma* for *nachtesse, yah?*" Abram asked her. Cerise tucked stray strands of hair back into her prayer bonnet and nodded quickly, her eyes surveying the classroom again. The garlands of green she had hung for Christmas were suddenly in the way for the building of the stage and the lighting seemed off somehow.

"If I can figure out how to do the staging here."

"There's lots of time before the pageant," Abram said, waving at Sadie to follow him outside and into the gently falling snow. "Don't go into it too hard now or you'll be exhausted on the day of the show."

"Uh, huh."

"Keep an eye on her," Abram said to his nephews.

"*Yah*, we will," Noah reassured him, starting to move the desks.

The next hour was consumed with moving furniture and Cerise determining what went where. Sarah Byler and her husband, Matthew, came by but Cerise sent them home, insisting that she was almost done for the day.

"It is getting late," she told the boys when she caught sight of the time. Guilt washed through her. "*Komme*, you must be *hungerich*."

To her surprise, the idea of dinner made them both perk up, as if she had announced a lottery win—or the Amish equivalent.

"Oh *yah. Yah*, I'm *hungerich*," Noah agreed, rubbing his stomach dramatically.

"Me too!" Daniel piped in, much too loudly.

Cerise's eyes narrowed. "What has gotten into you two *dienacht*?"

"*NIX*!" they chorused, bouncing toward the door of the schoolhouse. Sighing, Cerise grabbed her coat and cast a final look at the room, turned upside down with their planning.

Tomorrow's another day. It's not fair to keep the boys out so late and Abram is probably waiting for us now. Sadie is getting close to bedtime and Joshua isn't going to want me cooma home so late.

There were so many small things to consider these days, things she had never thought of in her life as a single woman, living in the city.

It had been a year of strenuous work, proving herself not only to the community but to herself. Joshua had not been lying about the amount of work involved with becoming a member of their district.

Many nights, she had laid awake in the small Dawdihaus that Joshua allowed her to rent from him, wondering if she wasn't cut out for the journey after all. The language had been harder to learn than the minister had suggested, the Ordnung more particular than she expected.

Despite what she had done to reclaim the children to Abram's care, there were still several families who didn't believe that a spinster social worker without a family could ever understand the core values of the Amish.

She remembered telling Abram all of her doubts as they shared dinner every night, after the children had gone to bed.

"You've already *komme* so far, Cerise. *Gott* has a plan for all of us. Don't you believe that still?"

She did believe that, even in the summer months where she learned to tend to Abram's farm, mucking out barns and milking dairy cows. She did work she had never believed she would ever do in her life.

Yet every moment of it was rewarding—and moving toward something.

And when she was finally up for baptism in the fall, everything suddenly fell into place, as if that had been the missing piece of her life all along.

The teaching job had come next, the offer waiting for her as the previous teacher had married and was soon expecting.

"You're so good with *kinner*," Bishop Speicher had said. "It would be a good fit for you and a steady income."

"But I'm not a teacher!"

"I beg to differ," the bishop had exclaimed. "I think you're a natural teacher. But there's only one way to find out. And if you don't like it, you can always give up the position."

The Bishop had proved a good prophet. Teaching had come easily to Cerise and the children loved her instantly.

Which was why the pageant was so important to her.

"Why are you running?" she demanded, noticing how the boys plunged though the snow ahead of her, kicking up the white dust as if they were in a huge hurry to return to the farm.

Again, they looked at one another but instead of answering, they sprinted ahead faster, leaving her to gather her skirt in her mittens and try to keep up.

Despite the darkness of the path, Cerise had long since learned the way from the schoolhouse back to the Hertzler house and even without following Noah and Daniel's footprints in the snow, she would have made it under the glow of the moonlight.

As she approached the brightly lit house, the boys had disappeared inside and she found herself staring at Abram on the front porch.

"I know, I know, it's late," she apologized before he could say a word. "I lost track of time."

He didn't speak, instead climbing down the steps to meet her, his azure eyes glowing against the backdrop of twinkling stars and white snow.

"Are you mad at me?" Cerise croaked, wishing he would say something.

"How could I ever be mad at you?" he asked, raising a hand to her cheek. "You are nothing but a wonder, always."

She laughed lightly and lowered her eyes. "Is Sadie asleep?"

"No. She's waiting for you. Just like always."

More shame moved through Cerise but before she could apologize again, Abram went on. "She knows this is a special *nacht*."

Cerise's brow furrowed in confusion.

"Oh no...did I miss someone's birthday?" she whispered. "Wait...we don't really do birthdays...do we?"

Abram chortled and shook his head. "It's not a birthday."

Confused, she peered at him. "I-I'm sorry. I'm at a loss. Help me out?" she begged. "What's so special about today?"

A smiled overtook his entire handsome face and he leaned closer, rubbing his nose against hers. "I met you exactly one year ago today."

Cerise blinked, shocked at the revelation. "*Wat*? Really?"

"A lot has happened since then, *yah*?"

"I'd say," she agreed with a giggle.

"But you know what I told myself back then? On those days right before Christmas?"

Cerise shook her head, relishing the warmth of his hand against her cheek, her eyes half closed.

"I told myself that by this time next year, your smile would grow even bigger, if possible. "Now I know we can't make that happen, not this *Chrischdaag,* but maybe for the New Year…if Bishop Speicher agrees? It's short notice but he might say yes."

Speechless, Cerise gawped at him.

"Are you…did you…?" she sputtered when she could find her voice.

"*Yah.* I'm asking you to be my *weib.* As soon as we possibly can."

Tears of happiness burned behind Cerise's eyes and she nodded, accepting Abram's embrace around her body.

"Did she say *yah?*" Daniel called out from the door.

"Danny!" Noah called out, pulling his brother back. Cerise laughed and sniffled, wiping her eyes as they broke apart.

"They knew about this!" she mumbled, shaking her head. "That's why they were acting that way!"

"I wanted to get their blessing before I asked you," Abram admitted. "Even though I knew what they were going to say —especially Sadie."

"You even asked Sadie?!"

"Of course! I couldn't ask her *bruders* and not ask her," Abram replied, his eyes widening. "Can you imagine?"

"*Nee*, I can't." Sighing, Cerise cupped Abram's cheeks and kissed him softly on the lips, drawing back. "You're a *gut mann*, Abram Hertzler. The *kinner* are very *glick* to have you. And so am I."

"Did she say yah, Abram?!" This time it was Sadie who shrieked the question out of the door, her entire blonde head poking through the screen as both her brothers pulled her back.

"I don't know," Abram called back as Cerise scoffed loudly.

"Don't you?" she replied, arching an eyebrow.

"*Nee*...you never answered me."

"Well then..." she dropped her arms and cocked her head to the side, a beautiful smile filling her entire face. "Let me tell you distinctly and clearly. *Yah*, Abram Hertzler. I will marry you. I want *nix* more than to be your *weib*."

Again, he embraced her, kissing the top of her head sweetly and turned toward the house.

"She said yes, *kinner*. Cerise is going to officially be your *aenti*."

Inside the house, the children cheered and Cerise allowed the tears to slip down her cheeks as Abram took her hand, leading her back toward the property where they would spend their second Christmas together—and third and fourth, and everyone thereafter. Cerise could barely wait to start the real rest of her life, the way it was always meant to be lived.

~*~*~

I do hope that you enjoyed reading my story.

May I suggest that you might also like to read my '*A Blessed Amish Christmas*' - *15 Book Box Set* that readers are loving!

Available on Amazon for just $0.99 or Free with Kindle Unlimited simply by clicking on the link below.

Click here to get your copy of 'A Blessed Amish Christmas - 15 Book Box Set' - Today!

Sample of Chapter One

The children had been unusually boisterous that morning, a fact that Greta could hardly fault them for. She had noticed the brilliant autumnal color changes on her way into the schoolhouse that morning, the fallen leaves gracing her walk to crunch at her feet, the crisp November air promising snow in the near future. The students were infected with the upcoming festive feeling, the knowledge that Christmas markets and celebratory plans were coming. It was perhaps a little bit too early to be making such plans, the weather was still a little too warm for such efforts, but with little eyes and little minds, they could hardly be expected to know the difference.

Still, she could not help but wish they would settle down some and heed her lessons with more attention. Greta spent so much of her evenings planning activities that would interest and keep the children engrossed. When they were not learning, she took it deeply and personally.

One child sat in the center row of the fourth-grade class, her eyes bright and clear as she tried to focus on Greta's own dark stare, even though all the others seemed more fixated on the events outside the schoolroom windows.

Finally, Greta had endured enough.

"My goodness, *kinner*," Greta chided them. "*Wat* has gotten into you all today?"

"My *vadder* said it's going to *schnee*!" Eva Byler giggled, nodding toward her brother. "Didn't he, David? Didn't he say that he could smell the *schnee* in the air?"

"He's never wrong about the first *schnee*," David agreed. "It would be a shame to miss it. We should be outside."

"How could you possibly miss it?" Greta teased them. "You'll have to walk *deheem* in it."

"You know what we mean." Eva sighed, splaying her hands over her desk. "Can't we take recess early and hope to catch the snowflakes before they fall to the ground?"

She stared pleadingly at the teacher, her youthful face full of promise and hope, neither of which Greta could easily dismiss. A part of her knew she had no business allowing such a treat but it was clear that she was not going to get anywhere with these children as they were.

With a sigh of resignation, she nodded and the children allowed a whoop of pleasure to escape their lips.

"You may take an extra ten minutes, no more," she said but her words were already falling on deaf ears.

"I want you all to bundle up," she called warningly as they flocked toward the doors. "Remember boots, hats—"

"*Yah, yah!*" they chorused, none truly listening as they rushed toward the entranceway, causing Greta to shake her blonde braid with another deep sigh. Only Nancy Sommers lingered behind, reluctant to rise and join the others as always, causing Greta to stare after her as she shuffled toward the door. The child appeared to be wasting time, as if her longer footsteps would account for the extra minutes somehow.

Greta bit on her lower lip a moment, unsure if she should do what she was considering. A part of her wanted the newcomer to make friends with the other children. She knew she should send Nancy outside to play and force the relationships that the girl appeared to fend off, but she also felt a kinship toward the outsider child. Perhaps it was the fact that Greta had always felt as if she were somewhat of an outcast herself in their small, Amish district. Growing up in Elkhart county, she had constantly been reminded that she was not as pretty as her counterparts with her "muddy" brown eyes and "stringy" blonde hair.

From a young age, Greta had recognized that she would not be courted and married off like her schoolmates, the boys regarding her more of a sister and the girls turning to her for motherly advice. It had been written in destiny that Greta would be a spinster even before her father had given up on the idea of her marrying, a fact that the girl had grown comfortable with early on.

She had always been enamored with the notion of being a schoolteacher, even if her father had been appalled by the notion at first. Ivan had attempted to talk her out of it—in the beginning.

"That is all fine and well until you're married, Greta," Ivan had protested. "But then you will have to settle down. A schoolteacher can't be married. You know that."

That had been over a decade earlier and Greta had been the longest running schoolteacher the district had seen to date.

Ivan was not proud of that fact but Greta took a certain pleasure in it.

It was for this reason that she tended to single out those who needed extra attention. Those like Nancy Sommers.

"Nancy," she called out as the girl reached the doorway. Gratefully, Nancy spun around, her eyes wide and thankful. "Will you *komme* here a moment and talk with me?"

"Am I in t-t-trouble?" Nancy asked worriedly. Greta chuckled and shook her head, waving a hand to gesture the girl toward the front of the classroom.

"*Nee*, of course not," she reassured the girl. "How can you ask something like that? You've done *nix* but excellent *warrick* since the moment you arrived here. In fact, that's what I want to discuss with you."

Blinking, Nancy inched closer, wariness overtaking her face as she neared.

"Unless you would rather be *autseid* with the others. It would do you *gut* to make *freind* with the other *kinner*, you know?"

Nancy exhaled, dropping her head toward the floor, scuffing her toe along the worn, wood planks as she moved along the woodstove. The days were still warm enough that the fire did not burn at full capacity but the windows needed to be fully closed and the doors sealed to allow for the draft to be kept out.

"I don't h-h-have anything in c-common with these *kinner*," she mumbled. The answer surprised Greta and she spoke her mind freely.

"Surely they aren't that much different than those from your own district," Greta insisted. "Didn't you have friends in your own district?"

Nancy did not respond but to give a short nod—one which did not convince Greta in any way.

"You just need to give them a chance. You'll see that they're not so different than any other *kinner* you know."

A pained expression overtook Nancy's face and Greta swiftly shifted topics, sensing that she was treading on sensitive ground. She was well-aware of the terms which had brought the girl to their community and she did not wish to stir up any bad memories. Moreover, it was not why she had asked the girl to stay behind.

"Your latest essay," Greta said primly. Nancy's head jerked up in concern.

"*W-wat* about it?"

"It's *wunderbar*! I'm very impressed with how well you can write."

A tentative smile formed on Nancy's lips as she met Greta's eyes.

"*Yah*?"

"Not that I'm surprised," Greta added. "Your *warrick* has been exemplary from the moment you arrived. Your last *Lehrer* must miss you a lot. She must be wondering when you'll return to her."

Nancy blushed furiously at the compliment and again stared down at her hands, apparently tongue-tied.

"There's no reason to be embarrassed," Greta told her. "I wish you would set an example for the rest of the students. They're more interested in making snowmen than they are in learning."

Nancy laughed lightly, folding and unfolding her hands in front of her skirt.

"I'm n-not an example f-f-for anyone," she mumbled.

"I don't believe that in the least," Greta announced, shaking her head. She stepped forward and placed her hands on the younger girl's shoulders, forcing Nancy to meet her eyes directly. "It's difficult *cooma* to a new home. Your *aenti* and *onkle* appreciate the *hilf*, I'm sure. Your *vadder* must be working very hard, a lot of hours, to assist them now."

Nancy's smile faded again but before she could speak, the door opened and Henry Eicher poked his head inside.

"How much longer can we stay outside?" he asked.

"I was just *cooma* to collect you," Greta informed him. "Collect the others. It's time to resume the lessons."

He groaned lightly but did not argue, turning to retrieve his classmates as Greta offered Nancy a smile.

"I have an *iwwerfalle* for you," the teacher whispered loudly, her eyes gleaming as she ushered the girl back toward her desk. Nancy eyed her uncertainly but followed Greta's direction as the other students filed back into the single-roomed schoolhouse, shedding off their boots and coats in a din of voices.

"Settle down now," Greta called out to them. "Get into your seats."

"There was no *schnee*," Eva complained. "Can't we stay out a little longer? Just until the snow falls."

"The snow might not fall," Greta said with a sigh.

"But our *vadder* said it would and our *vadder* is never wrong!"

"Not now," Greta told her. "Maybe it will *schnee* after *schul*."

"But I can smell it in the air!" Eva insisted.

"It won't go anywhere." Greta sighed. "Anyway, I have a special surprise for you."

Her words silenced the group, all eyes turning to her with interest.

"It isn't very often that I am blessed with *warrick* so moving, so delightful, that I think it should be shared with everyone," Greta explained, nodding toward Nancy. "Nancy, will you *komme* here for a moment, *pliese?*"

Nancy paled where she sat, shaking her head.

"*N-nee…*" she squeaked but Greta insisted.

"*Komme*," she said, extending her hand. "We're all *freind* here. There's no reason to be afraid."

The children began to murmur amongst themselves, confused by this latest turn of events and Greta shuffled toward her desk, retrieving Nancy's essay with a beam.

"This is what I want all of you to aspire toward," she told the group, holding up the pages. "This is how one should write from the heart and with such poise. I want you to listen to Nancy's words and hear how they ring true, *yah?*"

Nancy stood, shaking, at the head of the classroom as Greta joined her side, handing the essay to the girl.

"Go on, Nancy. Read it to them."

"*N-nee*, I don't w-want to," Nancy whimpered.

"It's all right, *liebling*. There's *nix* to fear here. Go on. I'm right here beside you."

She smiled encouragingly and Nancy's face turned opaque. Desperately, she looked around the building, the children's eyes fixated on her expectantly.

"Go on," Greta urged. "You should be proud, not embarrassed. Go ahead and read what you have written."

The children began to giggle amongst themselves, casting the new girl amused glances. Greta looked at them sternly but when she turned back to Nancy, there was fire in the child's face.

"*N-nee!*" Nancy howled, grabbing the pages from Greta's hands. "I s-s-said I don't w-w-want to!"

With that, the girl scampered toward the door, her coat forsaken as she rushed into the cool afternoon air, leaving Greta to gape after her in horror and confusion.

"Nancy!" Greta choked, hurrying toward the door but she had moved too slowly. The girl was halfway across the field by the time Greta approached the schoolhouse steps, showing no signs of returning. With a heavy heart, she turned back to her students, stunned and humiliated at what she had done.

"I can read my essay," Eva chirped. "But only if you let us go outside too!"

"Open your writing books." Greta frowned, her words barely rasps as she closed the door to block the chilled air. Shame overcame her as she realized that she had embarrassed the girl in a way that she had vowed never to do to a child.

I will make it right with Nancy, she promised, blinking away tears of contrition. *I will get her to trust me again.*

Click here to get your copy of 'A Blessed Amish Christmas - 15 Book Box Set' - Today!

A NOTE FROM THE AUTHOR

Dear Reader,

I do hope that you enjoyed reading '**Sweet Christmas Blessings**'

Possibly you even identify with the characters in some small way. Many of us presume to know God's will for our lives, and don't realize that His timing often does not match our own.

The foremost reason that I love writing about the Amish is that their lifestyle is diametrically opposed to the Western norm. The simplicity and purity evident there is so vastly refreshing that the story lines derived from them are suitable for everyone.

Be sure to keep an eye out for the next book which is coming soon.

Emma Cartwright

~

Thank You!

Thank you for purchasing this book. We hope that you have enjoyed reading it.

If you enjoyed reading this book **please may you consider leaving a review** — it really would help greatly to get the word out!

~

Newsletter

If you love reading sweet, clean, Amish Romance stories why not join Emma Cartwright's newsletter and receive advance notification of new releases and more!

Simply sign up here: http://eepurl.com/dgw2I5

And get your *FREE* copy of **Amish Unexpected Love**

~

Contact Me

If you'd simply like to drop us a line you can contact us at **emma@emmacartwrightbooks.com**

You can also connect with me on my new **Facebook page**.

I will always let you know about new releases on my Facebook page, so it is worth liking that if you get the chance.

LIKE EMMA'S FB PAGE HERE

I welcome your thoughts and would love to hear from you!

I will then also be able to let you know about new books coming out along with Amazon special deals etc